LIZZIE'S
LEAVING

LIZZIE'S LEAVING

Joan Lingard

Hamish Hamilton

For Sarah Lingard Tierney

HAMISH HAMILTON LTD

Published by the Penguin Group
27 Wrights Lane, London w8 5tz, England
Penguin Books USA Inc, 375 Hudson Street, New York, New York 10014, USA
Penguin Books Australia Ltd, Ringwood, Victoria, Australia
Penguin Books Canada Ltd, 10 Alcorn Avenue, Toronto, Ontario, Canada, m4v 3b2
Penguin Books (NZ) Ltd, 182–190 Wairau Road, Auckland 10, New Zealand

Penguin Books Ltd, Registered Offices: Harmondsworth, Middlesex, England

First published in Great Britain 1995 by Hamish Hamilton Ltd

Text copyright © 1995 by Joan Lingard

1 3 5 7 9 10 8 6 4 2

The moral right of the author has been asserted

Typeset by Datix International Limited, Bungay, Suffolk
Printed in England by Clays Ltd, St Ives plc
Set in 13/15pt Monophoto Bembo

British Library Cataloguing in Publication Data
CIP data for this book is available from the British Library

ISBN 0–241–13529–X

ONE

'*W*hat are you doing?'

'What do you think I'm doing? Packing! I'm putting clothes into bags – all my clothes! Or all the ones I want to keep, anyway. You can have anything that's left or else give it to the Oxfam shop.' Lizzie crammed another tee-shirt into the corner of the duffel bag, then she sat back, and frowned. She pressed the tips of her fingers against her temples. Trainers. Where were her trainers? She wriggled underneath the bed to re-emerge, red-faced but triumphant, with the two shoes in question, plus a red sock, a hairbrush, a broken-toothed comb – rather disgusting-looking, kind of gungy, down at the roots – the bus pass she'd lost for most of last term, and the stub end of a roll of Polo mints. Dustballs clung to her short, curly, dark red hair. She sneezed.

Alice continued to lean against the door jamb, her eyes glistening behind their round spectacles.

'Where are you going?'

'Where do you think I'm going? To my father's, of course.'

'Does he want you?' Alice's wide blue eyes roamed until they lighted on an opened letter lying on the desk under the window, then they narrowed.

'Of course he wants me! Do you think I'd go otherwise? For someone who's meant to be brainy you can be right dumb at times. He said *please* do come. We would love to have you.

'Her, too?'

'Her, too. So I'm going.' Lizzie rammed the trainers on top of the contents of the duffel bag. She tugged at the zip. It gave up half way across.

'How do you know you'll like him? Or her?'

'I'm sure I'll like him. He sounds really, really nice, from his letters. *And* his voice. I spoke to him on the phone yesterday.'

'He wasn't nice enough to marry our mum.'

'They were only seventeen. Still at school.'

'Doesn't mean they couldn't have got married.'

'I wouldn't fancy getting married in two years.'

'I should think not!' The idea horrified Alice. Lizzie married? She changed her mind about boys every other day.

'Anyway, these things are complicated, Alice. And beyond *your* comprehension.'

'Yah boo to you too! Well, I'm glad he didn't. Marry her. For then she wouldn't have been able to marry Peter. And I wouldn't be here.'

'Think what a blessing that would have been!'

Alice showed the tip of her tongue. 'Does she know?'

'I told her last night.'

Alice went out on to the landing. 'Mum!' she yelled

over the banisters. 'Lizzie's leaving. Can I have her room?'

There was no reply. Alice threw her leg over the banister and slid down until she hit the newel post, which was wobbly. She had been forbidden to slide down the banisters. Expressly forbidden. In those words. By her mother. Her father would have said, 'Hey, knock it off, Alice! If you break that post we won't be able to find money for another.'

Her mother and father were at the table. Her father, Peter, was at home for breakfast, which was unusual. It must be on account of Lizzie's leaving. He had a newsagent's shop and had to go out at six every morning to do the papers. He'd have left his helper, Mrs Kelly, in charge. He was eating a piece of burnt toast (he kept saying they must get a toaster) and eyeing the morning paper. (Marge, his wife, Alice and Lizzie's mother, hated him reading at the table.) Marge was spooning grey sludge into the half-open mouth of Jamie, the youngest in the family. A rim of grey outlined Jamie's lips and some of the mixture had dropped into the gutter of his bib. Johnny, who had recently celebrated his fourth birthday (with a horde of barbaric, deafening small boys) was running a yellow dump truck (one of his presents) up and down the table, manoeuvring it deftly between plates and saucers and the milk bottle and the cornflake packet. 'Vroom, vroom!' he was crying, his thin reedy voice rising like a seagull's.

The two parents were attempting to carry on a conversation over the top of it all.

'If she wants to go then we'll have to let her,'

Marge was saying. Miserably. 'We can't forcibly hold her here.'

'You could tie her to the bed post,' suggested Alice.

'I expect she'll just go for the summer,' said Peter.

'She says she's going for good. Stop spitting, Jamie!' His mother wagged the spoon at him. 'I hope she does!' Her mood was changing, becoming angry. 'Go for good. It'll be good for the rest of us.'

'You don't really mean that, Marge.'

'I certainly do. I'm fed up to the back teeth with her. She's been ghastly for the past six months. Ever since —'

'She found her father,' said Alice.

'Shut up, Alice!' said her mother, turning back to her husband. 'You're fed up with her too. Go on, Peter, admit it!'

'It's a phase.'

'Some phase! I'm sick of being told that. This one's gone on far too long. She's downright impossible.'

'Can I have her room?' put in Alice.

Her request was ignored.

'Don't you think you should go up and have a word with her, Marge?' said Peter.

'Oh, I suppose so!' Marge threw up her hands and got to her feet.

Lizzie looked up as the door was edged open after a perfunctory tap.

'Can I come in?'

Lizzie said neither yes nor no. Her mother was coming anyway. She sat down on the bed.

'I can't believe this is actually happening,' Marge said.

'Well, it is,' said Lizzie, in a voice that would have cooled boiling water on a hot day.

'I could stop you going. But I won't, of course.'

'There wouldn't be any point, would there? I'd just go when I was older.'

'I can understand you wanting to see your father.'

'You kept me from him long enough.'

'*I* kept you from him? That's not fair and you know it! It was he who walked away. He turned his back on us. What do you think my life was like, going out to work with a small baby? Taking you to a nursery in the mornings. Living in two rooms with a gas ring and a shared loo.'

'He was young.'

'So was I. He didn't help support you.'

'He was a student. How could he?'

'I'd have liked to have gone to art college and been a student too.'

'If you hadn't had three more children you might have got there by now.'

The kids had taken up all Marge's time and sapped her energy, she'd said so herself. She'd wanted a large family. It was not a road Lizzie intended to travel.

'Thanks for the sympathy!'

'It's not *my* fault you didn't get to college. I didn't *ask* to be born.'

'I'm not trying to lay the blame at *your* door. I was happy the day you were born, in spite of everything. I wanted you. You know that, don't you?'

'Yes,' said Lizzie in a muffled voice. She felt as if her throat was swollen and hoped she wasn't getting laryngitis. She bent over to re-tie her lace. She didn't want to look at her mother's face. She couldn't bear to. For she had to go. She just *had* to. This was her chance, and he might not ask her again.

She was aware of her mother getting up.

'Just remember that I love you, Lizzie.'

'You told me once that love in itself was not enough. You said you and Mark loved one another.' Lizzie lifted her head now.

'That's true.' Her mother sighed. 'I hope you won't be disappointed by him, dear.' She touched the top of Lizzie's head, and left the room.

Of course I won't be disappointed, thought Lizzie, and blew her nose violently. She didn't expect him to be a paragon. Faultless. He'd just be an ordinary man. Her *father*.

'I hope he likes purple,' said Alice, as Lizzie came in to the kitchen wearing new jeans, purple socks, a purple blouse and purple eye make-up. 'It makes you look lugubrious. As if you were going to a wake.'

'Shut up, Alice!'

'This family's dead boring, so it is,' said Alice, showering cornflakes into a bowl. 'It keeps repeating itself. "Shut up, Alice,"' she mimicked, aping Lizzie's voice.

'Breakfast, Lizzie?' Peter set about clearing a place.

'No, thank you. I'll just have a cup of tea.' Lizzie upended the teapot. A thin, brackish trickle emerged. She set down the teapot as if this was only what she'd expected.

'You could make some more,' said her mother.

'I'll not bother. I'll have coffee on the train.'

Jamie opened his mouth and blew out a gritty grey bubble. It sprayed his mother's face and she laughed and wriggled her nose at him and said, 'You little devil!'

Johnny, vying for attention, brought the dump truck up the side of the teapot, intensifying his vroom vrooms. On the way down his hand knocked against the milk bottle.

'That's enough of that!' His father removed the truck from Johnny's hand before starting to mop up the milk. 'And you can just stop that noise or else leave the table!' Johnny had started to bawl.

'I'll be on my way, then,' said Lizzie.

'Have you got enough money?' asked her mother. 'Alice, fetch me my purse.'

'Where is it?' asked Alice, through a mouthful of cornflakes. Their mother's purse could be anywhere from the top of the loo to the inside of the fridge.

'I don't need any money,' said Lizzie. 'He's sent me more than enough.'

'Wow! Is he wealthy?' asked Alice. 'How much did he send?'

'Never you mind!'

'Maybe you'll get your own personal video and camcorder.'

Lizzie ignored her sister and drifted towards the door.

'I'll run you to the station.' Peter got to his feet.

'You don't have to.'

'I know that. But I will.'

'I might as well come too.' Alice pushed aside her

bowl. 'Make sure you don't chicken out at the last minute.'

'Me come too!' yelled Johnny.

'You can just stay here,' said his father.

'Give me a kiss at least, love,' said Marge. 'Before you go.'

Lizzie proffered her face, keeping it turned to one side. Her mother's kiss glanced off her ear.

'You know you can always come back.'

'To this?' Lizzie, looked round at the clothes dangling from the pulley overhead, the scattered toys that reduced the floor to an obstacle race, the piles of yellowing newspapers waiting to be thrown out. 'It's like a zoo.'

Colour flamed in Marge's cheeks. 'You see what I mean, Peter! She's impossible.'

'I didn't mean to say that,' muttered Lizzie. 'Tell her, will you?'

'Why did you, then?' asked Alice, squinting along the track for signs of life. ·

'Hush up, Alice,' said Peter. And then to Lizzie, 'I'm sure she'd know that. She'd realise you were feeling, well, you know —' He shrugged, unwilling to commit himself to a definite word.

'On edge,' supplied Alice.

'I am not on edge,' Lizzie informed her. 'I feel perfectly calm.'

'It would be understandable if you were,' said Alice. 'On edge. Teetering.' She held out her arms and wobbled as if she were losing her balance.

'Here comes the train,' said Peter. 'Get back, Alice!'

There was a stir amongst the waiting travellers as they retrieved their bits and pieces of luggage and shuffled forward. Lizzie hoisted up her rucksack and duffel bag.

'Now, remember,' said Peter, 'if it doesn't work out you're to come home. Straight away. Okay?'

The train juddered to a halt and doors flew open. Passengers began to pile out. Lizzie kissed Alice and Peter quickly in turn.

'Write!' commanded Alice.

'You too!' said Lizzie, her eyes already turning away from them. 'I'd better get on.'

As she moved along the platform to the nearest compartment door, Peter called after her, 'Good luck. Lizzie! And give us a ring when you get there.'

'And don't talk to any strange men,' added Alice. 'Apart from your father.'

TWO

The train was an inter-city express, and busy, but Lizzie managed to find a place by the window in one of the airline-type seats. She stowed on the rack overhead the two bags that contained all the worldly possessions she wanted to keep. When she'd gone through her clothes she had found there were surprisingly few. She had wanted to slough off her wardrobe along with her old life.

'No taking back!' Alice had cried, gathering up armfuls of tee-shirts and sweaters.

Lizzie leant over on to one hip and eased her father's last letter from the back pocket of her jeans, the one in which he'd asked her to come and stay. He'd written on linen-coloured notepaper with a firm, flowing hand – artistic, she couldn't help thinking – in brownish-black ink.

'We've got a lot to catch up on, you and I. Years and years. Fifteen! I want to know everything about you. It would be great to have you here . . .'

She let her eyes slide from the letter to the window.

They had left the city behind, the rigid rows of houses, the factories, the gaunt high rises, the litter, the dirt; were rolling now through bright green fields. Poppies grew in red splashes. Brown and white cows grazed. The world looked so fertile. So bright. So strangely new. She felt as if she were seeing it for the first time. She hugged her arms across her body. This would be a summer to remember. And she was going to start a diary, so that she wouldn't forget any little detail. She'd never kept one before, unlike Alice, who'd been scribbling in notebooks since she could hold a pencil.

She'd been dreaming about her father for a long time. When she was small she'd imagined him in shining armour riding a black horse. Galloping through the night. Coming for her. Bending down to scoop her up, and away they'd go, the horse's tail streaming out behind them in the wind. Other times, he'd been a pop star. A prince. An athlete. Winning the gold medal at the Olympic Games. The crowd cheering. And there he would be, standing on the rostrum with his head inclined to receive the medal, and at that very moment he would turn to look into the crowd. At *her*.

For years the only thing she'd known about him was his first name. MARK. Four letters. She'd written them over and over again on pieces of paper, in capital letters, and small, in large italics, in a backward sloping hand, forward, up and down. She'd written her own name underneath his.

MARK
LIZZIE

They didn't have a single letter in common. She'd stared at the two words until they began to blur in front of her eyes.

It wasn't much to know, just his name. But it had been enough for her to be able to talk to him in her head. 'Hello, Mark, this is Lizzie here – your daughter Lizzie.'

She'd asked her mother if he was handsome. At the very least she could tell her that!

'Oh, I suppose you'd say he was handsome!' her mother had conceded. 'And charming. He was what my mother called a charming boy, until he pulled out on me. He charmed everyone!'

On her fifteenth birthday Lizzie had demanded to know more. His full name, for a start. 'I have a right to it. He's my father, isn't he? The other half of my identity. I feel that part of me's blank.'

Her mother held up her hands. 'All right! It was Mark Anthony Wheeler.'

'Mark Anthony,' Lizzie repeated.

'His mother had a funny sense of humour. I never did care for her much. I'm sure she put him against me.'

'*My* grandmother! You're talking about *my* grandmother! Do you realise I've got a grandmother I haven't seen? And probably all sorts of other relatives.'

'I thought you'd no time for relatives? When we have the aunts over you make yourself scarce.'

Lizzie had not bothered to answer that one.

'Tea, coffee?' She heard the rattle of the refreshment

trolley. She bought coffee and a bacon, lettuce and tomato sandwich, but when she tried to eat she found she had little appetite. Her stomach was doing back flips with excitement. Well, no wonder! She was going to meet her father for the very first time.

Once she'd known his full name, the rest had been fairly easy. She'd wheedled out of her mother all the other details she could give her: where he'd been born, had lived, gone to school, to college. She'd gone to the public library and rifled through telephone directories. She found a Mark A. Wheeler living in a town only twenty miles away from where her mother and father had met.

She wrote to him. 'Could you be *the* Mark Anthony Wheeler who knew my mother Marge Halliday, as she was then, at school? I am her daughter. I am fifteen years old.'

'Why should he answer now?' Alice had demanded. 'After disowning you at birth. Before birth. He probably won't reply.'

But he had.

The train stopped, and more people got on. Lizzie was forced to lift her rucksack. A large woman with spreading thighs and bulging shopping bags plumped down beside her.

'Whew, it's hot, isn't?'

Lizzie had not noticed.

The woman began to chat. 'Going on holiday, are you?'

'No, I'm going home.'

'Home? Then you must have been on holiday.'

'Not exactly.' Lizzie had a sudden desire to speak,

to tell the world. 'I've been living for some years with my mother and stepfather, you see, and now I'm going to stay with my father. And stepmother,' she added.

'Ah, you're from a broken home, then?' The woman was sympathetic. 'Common nowadays, I'm afraid.'

There had been no home to break, but Lizzie did not tell her that. She had no wish to reveal everything.

'So you're kind of caught between the two? Shuttling back and forth?'

'Oh, no, it's not like that. Not at *all* like that. This is to be permanent, this move to my father's.'

'Come for the summer,' he'd written, 'and then we'll see.' We'll see how we get on, he'd meant. Which was perfectly reasonable. She wouldn't have expected him to say come for ever and ever when they hadn't even met! The idea was perfectly ludicrous, as she'd pointed out to Alice, who'd said he was hedging his bets.

'Get on well together, do you, you and your dad?' asked the woman.

'Very well.' Lizzie opened her bag. 'Would you like to see a picture of him?'

The woman leaned over. 'He's a good looker all right! Young too, to have a daughter like you.'

'He's thirty-three.'

'Must have had you when he was only – what?'

'Eighteen. Just turned.'

'That's young. Nice house he's got. And a big garden, from the looks of it.'

'He's an interior designer, his wife Candice is as well. They're terribly successful. They travel all over the world.'

'Got any other nippers, have they?'

'A girl, Cressida. She's seven.' Lizzie produced another photograph. 'That's her, Cressida – my half-sister.'

'Candice and Cressida. Fancy names. Got any halves or steps on the other side?'

'Three halves. Two little brothers, and a sister aged eleven, called Alice. She's what you'd call a precocious kid.'

'No pictures of them?'

'They're all packed away. In my duffel bag.'

The woman got up for the next stop. 'It's been nice talking to you. Hope everything works out.'

Lizzie took out the very first letter her father had written her, in reply to hers. She had read it so often that the paper was creased and the writing smudged in places.

'I've often thought about you and wondered what you looked like, but I didn't get in touch. I don't know if I was right or wrong in doing that but I thought it best not to interfere in your mother's life after we split up. Or to confuse you, by suddenly appearing, especially after I heard on the grapevine that Marge had married. She needed to have the chance to make a fresh start without me making an appearance in the picture.'

Lizzie put the letter away. She had four more stops to go. She went to the lavatory three times between the penultimate and last stops. She stood in the smelly little compartment feeling sick. What if she didn't like him? What if *he* didn't like *her*?

It was noon when she stepped down from the train. High noon, Alice would have said, had she been here. Thank goodness she wasn't! What a pain in the neck that child could be. She had a crack for every occasion. 'Go away, Alice,' said Lizzie, in her head, mentally flapping her aside as one might a buzzing fly.

THREE

*A*lice spent the rest of the morning settling into Lizzie's room. It was a nice sunny room with space not only for a desk but a bookcase and a small settee, and it had a window that looked over the back garden. It was a room Alice had long coveted. Her own room, until now, had been a box room with a skylight window. She'd had to stand on her bed to look out at the world and even then had been able to see only roofs and chimney pots. She liked roofs and chimney pots, the way they jutted out and made patterns against the sky, though she preferred trees and plants, on the whole.

'Now it's only temporary, remember, Alice!' her mother had said. 'Lizzie might well be back after the summer. I can't see them wanting her full-time. She's got to come back for school, after all.'

'She said she could go to school there.'

'Did *he* say that?'

'I think so.' Alice had been deliberately vague. She had not actually seen any of the letters; Lizzie had kept them out of her arm's reach and read aloud selected parts. Her mother's eyes had been red; she'd been crying while they were away at the station. Alice had reached up and given her a hug.

'Don't you follow her example when you're fifteen, Alice!'

Alice had no intention of following anyone's example. Not that she had an unknown father to run off to. She presumed she didn't. No, she was pretty sure Peter was her real father. Everyone said she was his spitting image. Peter said that meant if you spat you saw your image in it. He was full of interesting bits of information. He had plenty of that kind of reading material in the shop.

Alice took Lizzie's books out of the bookcase and replaced them with her own, then she arranged her collections of stamps, shells, agates and fossils on the shelves, and unpinned Lizzie's posters so that she could put up one of the firmament showing the stars in the northern hemisphere and a sequence of beautifully coloured pictures of the Antarctic. She was considering becoming a geophysicist (among other things) when she grew up and the Antarctic was on her list of places to go to.

When she'd sorted out her possessions and put her clothes in the drawers, she vacuumed the carpet and dusted all the ledges. (She was the tidiest in the family and from time to time would tackle even the kitchen.)

With everything in order, she took out her journal and wrote up today's entry.

'Lizzie left home today. She's a bit of a twit, really. Going off to stay with total strangers! You wouldn't catch me doing that. I know she's been writing to him for six months but you can't tell what someone's like from what they write, can you? He could be a monster. So could she. Another version of the Wicked Stepmother. Masquerading under all that showy blond hair and soft smile. They seem to be a family of smilers. Grinning out of their photographs, showing off their snow-white teeth. How could Frizzie Lizzie fit in there? The trouble with Lizzie is she's too proud ever to admit she's made a mistake. She and Mum are far too alike. They fight like cat and dog. This last year has been absolutely ghastly with the two of them going at it ding-dong and Lizzie smouldering in-between-times like a volcano that's about to blow its lid off. Sometimes you could see the steam coming out of her head. Dad said she was going through an identity crisis! I saw her writing Lizzie Wheeler on a piece of paper, over and over, and then she covered it with her arm when she saw I was looking and told me to stop spying on her. I thought she was going to cry at the station. Kids! said Dad, when we were going back to the car. I said I didn't know why he'd bothered having so many. We called at the wine shop on the way back and Dad bought a bottle of red wine to cheer Mum up. You don't think all this makes your mother happy, do you? he said. I don't see why people have to get their knickers in a twist so much. Why can't they play it cool? Mum's downstairs now with her friend Ginny drinking the wine and going over and over everything that's happened. Where did I go wrong? she's asking Ginny. I mean what's the point? Where'll it get her? It's history, isn't it? Past.

Like the Second World War. It can't be changed now. And Lizzie's gone, at least for the present.'

After lunch, Alice did some work in her garden. She had a plot at the back, beside the wall, where she grew vegetables and herbs. She helped feed the family. They needed all the help they could get, in her view. She particularly liked her rows of herbs. Rosemary, marjoram, coriander, dill, mint, oregano, thyme. Their names pleased her, and their smells, when she rubbed the leaves between her fingers and when they were cooking in the pot. She liked growing things, grubbing around in the earth.

Marge and Peter had taken the little kids to the park. They'd asked her if she'd wanted to come but she hadn't. She didn't like the park, especially on a Saturday afternoon. Too many small kids with balls.

When the telephone rang she dropped her fork and raced up the path, leaping over a sprawled trike and an assembly of small cars. She ducked under the washing drooping from its line and went into the house. In her haste she almost knocked the phone off the shelf.

'Hello. Oh, it's you, Carol . . .' Her voice dropped. Carol was one of Lizzie's numerous friends. Lizzie always went around with squads of people and they rang at all hours of the day and night and the phone would be gummed up for hours until their mother would go in and explode at her.

When Peter had asked Lizzie if she wouldn't miss her friends she'd shrugged and said she'd make new ones. And, besides, Carol and Helen and Shona could always come and visit her. She wasn't going *that* far away, only a train ride.

'No, I thought it might have been Lizzie,' said Alice to Carol. She glanced over at the grandmother clock, which said twenty past two. 'She said she'd ring when she got there. Yes, she went. No, she didn't change her mind at the last minute. She should have been there by now. Guess the train could have been late. Or else she's forgotten. You know Lizzie . . .'

FOUR

*H*e was waiting at the end of platform, scanning the crowd. She knew him straight away, the way his thick dark hair lifted from his forehead, the way he smiled, and his eyes crinkled. He appeared familiar to her: that was the extraordinary thing. But maybe it wasn't so extraordinary. He *was* her father.

He saw her too, at the very same moment. It was instant recognition. She ran forward, her duffel bag bumping against her knees, her rucksack jumping up and down on her shoulders.

'Lizzie! It *must* be Lizzie!' He took hold of her shoulders and studied her face. 'You're the image of your mother!'

Lizzie knew that, but would have preferred it if he had known her only for herself. He had rejected her mother, after all. The knowledge jiggled inside her head, demanding to be remembered. But it didn't mean he would reject *her*.

He took her to a coffee bar nearby. 'To give us

time to get acquainted a little before you take on the rest of the family. Cressy's dying to meet you.'

And Candice? wondered Lizzie. No mention of Candice. What would she be thinking as she waited for them to arrive? Whatever *he* says, Alice had said, you can't expect *her* to be totally over the moon. Lizzie wished Alice would leave her alone. What was it about her little sister that she went with you inside your head?

It was a glitzy coffee bar, with chrome fitments and marble tops veined in green and white. The green and yellow glass lamps were shaped like petals. Very twenties-looking. Mark – her very own father – had been the designer. Lizzie found everything beautiful, exactly to her liking.

'I'm glad,' he said. 'It's good that we have the same taste.'

He ordered an expresso and she, encouraged by him, decided on a large cappuccino with a strawberry tart. Now that her stomach had stopped somersaulting she'd become aware that she was starving.

They faced one another across the table.

'You're actually here, Lizzie!' He shook his head. 'I can't quite believe it.'

Nor could she. It felt like an extenuation of her dreams. She felt shy now. And perhaps so did he, just a little. He might even have been nervous, when he'd been waiting for her train to arrive. He might have had second thoughts. Was this a good idea, he might have been thinking as he'd stood on the platform watching her train approach. He might even have been tempted to turn tail and run.

'So, how's your mother?'

'Fine.'

'She sounded just the same when I spoke to her on the phone last night.' (From the top landing, Lizzie had heard her mother in the hall below, very cool, very polite. 'Maybe it's time you took over some responsibility for your child, Mark. After all, she *is* your child too, something you've chosen to ignore for the past fifteen years.')

Lizzie ate her strawberry tart, trying not to wolf it too quickly. He must find her boring, answering in monosyllables. And she so badly wanted to appear *interesting*. Her throat felt dry. Almost sore, the way that it had since she'd decided to come and see him. She took a sip of coffee, wished she could think of something arresting to say.

'How many kids did you say Marge has now?' he asked.

'Four altogether, including me, of course. Three are Peter's.' And I am yours, thought Lizzie, feeling light-headed, in spite of the food. *Yours!*

'Peter all right?'

'Yes, he's okay.' Lizzie shrugged. She hadn't come here to talk about *them*. Peter had adopted her when he married her mother, but she didn't want to have to tell her real father that. But, suddenly, thinking about Peter and his good-natured face, she felt suddenly guilty, and added lamely, 'He's very nice.'

'What does he do?'

She hesitated. 'He's got a newsagent's.' She knew her voice was on the defensive side, though she didn't want it to be. 'He was made redundant, you see, from the bank.'

'I guess your mother doesn't work with all those kids to take care of?' Mark drained his coffee cup, shifted a little on his leather stool. Then he looked up. His gaze was steady. 'We were very young, your mother and —'

'Oh, yes, I know,' said Lizzie rapidly. 'I understand, really I do.' She wanted to tell him he didn't have to apologise to her, she didn't have to forgive him. Or did she? She wasn't sure about that. Sometimes, during the last six months, she'd felt very angry with him. She'd railed at him in her head? *Why didn't you come and find me? We've wasted fifteen years!* But she couldn't be angry now, seeing him for the first time in her life, and wanting so desperately to get on with him. You couldn't start a relationship with someone by attacking him.

'We were seventeen.' He sighed. 'Boys aren't as mature as girls at that age.'

Lizzie nodded. Zac Hornbeam, who lived next door back home, was the same age as she was, and she found him young.

'Not that I'm trying to say it was her fault or she should have known better or anything like that!'

'Of course not.'

'I wasn't ready to settle down. And she wouldn't — '

Have an abortion? Was that what he'd been going to say? She couldn't really blame him if that was what he'd suggested, then. Still at school, thinking his world was about to open up. With no money. His mother against it. Threatening to show him the door. Cut him off without a penny. Not that she had too many pennies, from all accounts. From Marge's account.

Which was the only one Lizzie had. Mrs Wheeler was a widow and had brought up Mark on her own. Never get entangled with an only son and a widowed mother, Marge had advised Lizzie.

'It's all water under the bridge,' said Lizzie. 'I mean, it happened before I was born.' She'd made him smile again.

'You're a sweet girl.'

'*Sweet?*' Lizzie heard the dratted Alice's voice in her ear again. *You sweet? Ha, ha. Wait till he really gets to know you! Wait till you have one of your famous Mount Vesuvius eruptions and the hot lava hits the ceiling!*

'*You* seem mature for your age. I can't believe you're only fifteen.'

Lizzie flushed, pleased by the compliment. She felt she'd grown up several years in the course of the last few hours.

'Come on!' He jumped up, held out his hand. 'Let's go home and meet Candice and Cressy!'

FIVE

*A*lice looked up as the side gate squeaked. Peter had been meaning to oil it for ages.

'Hi!' said Zac, and came loping across the grass, all gangly arms and legs.

'Mind the rake!' she called, too late. He had already stubbed his toe on it and only just caught it in time before the end hit him on the forehead. He was accident prone, was Zac, and held the record in the street for the number of times he'd been to Accident and Emergency. He had scars all over his body to show for it.

He hopped the rest of the way, then collapsed on the ground, nursing his toe.

'Lizzie get away?' he asked.

'No, she's hiding in the attic.'

He picked off a leaf of mint and crushed it idly between his fingers to smell it. Alice frowned at him.

'It's all right, Allie, I'm not going to vandalise your precious garden.'

Alice hated being called Allie. Dirt flew under her fork and he had to move back a bit.

'Mind your lettuces!' he cried. 'You're getting soil on them. You'll need to vacuum them.'

She didn't deign to reply. But he was right: she had got dirt on her lettuces. She didn't bother to remove it, however; she wouldn't give him the satisfaction of seeing her do it.

'You'll miss her, won't you?' he said.

'Who? Lizzie? You must be joking! It's great having some peace and quiet.'

'It does seem quiet round here.' Zac sighed and lay back on the grass. He'd always had a soft spot for Lizzie (he was soft in the head, Alice considered, at least on that score), but he'd never had any encouragement from her, not in *that* way. Lizzie said he was like a brother to her. The Boy Next Door. Lizzie liked boys with a bit more razzmatazz to them. Unsuitable boys, in the eyes of Marge. And Alice, too. They were bores mostly, with nothing to talk about. They slunk around looking trendy (in *their* eyes) and emitted the odd grunt.

'I got some new stamps today,' said Zac, 'from the Baltic states. One from Latvia and one from Estonia.'

'Got any doubles? I'll swap you.'

'Could let you have a couple.'

'Great!'

They entered into a philatelic discussion; they were both keen collectors and occasionally Zac went to stamp fairs. When he could raise the money. He'd said he would take Alice sometime and she reminded him of that now.

'Okay! If your mother says yes.'

28

When the phone rang Alice leapt up and fled back across the grass, with Zac at her heels and threatening to overtake her.

'Don't trip me, Zachary Hornbeam!' she warned.

They skidded into the hall and she seized the receiver.

'Hello.' She looked across at Zac and raised her thumb. 'So you finally remembered us, did you? We're honoured. How's it going, then?'

Alice listened for a few seconds, then covered the receiver with her hand and said to Zac, '*He*'s wonderful, you'll be glad to hear. So easy to talk to. So sympathetic. Just like she imagined. And has she done a lot of imagining!' Alice listened again, said, '*She*'s wonderful. So welcoming. So attractive.' Listened again. 'And Cressy is simply de-lightful. Not at all like me, Lizzie says. I should hope not!' Listened again for a long time, then at the end said into the receiver, 'Well, I'm glad everything's so perfect, Frizzie Lizzie. The house. Your room. Even the garden. Full of roses,' she said in an aside to Zac. 'No, I was just saying to Zac that the garden's full of roses. Yes, he's here. Sends his L-U-V. Carol called. Shona called. They'd nothing much to say. They never do, do they? No, I guess you'd better not ring his phone bill up too high, even though he is filthy rich. Yeah, I'll tell them.'

Alice put down the receiver.

'Sounds as if she likes it, then,' said Zac gloomily.

When the rest of the family came home, Alice was submitted to a barrage of questions. She grumbled that it was like facing the Spanish Inquisition.

'Though they probably tore their fingernails out as well.'

Peter wanted to know how Lizzie had found Mark. 'Did she feel awkward with him? Does she like him?'

'It's as if they've known one another all their lives.'

'That's good,' said Peter heavily.

Marge wanted to know how Lizzie had found Candice. She said the name as if she'd bitten into a bad plum and couldn't spit it out.

'Candice has taken Lizzie to her bosom. No sign of vipers in it. Or poisoned apples, either. Doesn't appear to be a case of Enter the Wicked Queen! So much the worse! It would have been more interesting.'

'Be serious for a minute, Alice!'

'I am being serious. Lizzie said Candice was lovely, beautifully dressed, vivacious, amusing, intelligent. Want any more? And Candice thinks Lizzie's the greatest thing since sliced bread. And the house is out of this world. Orbiting in space.'

'All right, all right, we get the picture!' Marge tugged her tee-shirt straight. It had a large brown streak on its white front where Jamie had rested a dripping choc ice. She glared at Alice. 'You might have washed the lunch dishes.'

'I've been slaving in the garden *all* afternoon. Working my fingers to the bone to provide food —'

Marge began to bang dirty pots about.

'I'll wash them,' said Peter, edging her out of the way.

'It's all right for Mark,' said Marge. '*He* was able to pursue his career, do what *he* wanted.'

'You've told us that before,' said Alice. 'Anyway,

you're always telling us life's not fair.' She dodged quickly out of the way.

She went up to her room to put her two newly-acquired stamps into her album. Zac had given them to her as a present and had not extracted anything in return. And she had got him to promise, lick his finger, cross his heart, that he'd take her to the very next stamp collectors' fair. She was going to ask her dad if he'd let her help out in the shop, now that it was the holidays. For some financial reward, of course. She would save the money to spend at the fair.

She had left her door ajar to get some through draft. The afternoon had been warm and close. She cocked her ear. They were talking in the kitchen, must have left their door open too. It was not a house in which people shut doors.

'Peter,' her mother was saying, 'I'm worried about Alice.'

Oh, no! Surely Marge was not going to start worrying about *her* now that she no longer had Lizzie to torment herself over. Mothers! Alice got up and went out on to the landing. She knew very well before she listened that eavesdroppers never heard any good of themselves.

'She's *such* a loner, Peter. I mean, she doesn't seem to have any friends of her own age. If I suggest she asks someone home to tea she says she doesn't want to. And she's never asked to anyone else's house. It's all to do with her being so brainy and put up a couple of classes. We should never have agreed to that. It means she's by far the youngest in the class and socially less mature than the others.'

'Keep your voice down, Marge! She'll hear you.'

'She went back out to the garden, I'm sure she did. It doesn't seem natural to me, spending all that time *gardening* when you're eleven years old.'

Alice closed the door of her room quietly. It was perfectly *natural* to garden. What could be more *natural* than growing things? It was a lot more natural than chucking balls about or batting them over a net. Really, there were an awful lot of things her mother didn't understand. As for being a loner, how could you be *alone* in this family? And she talked to all sorts of people all the time. There was Mrs Moon, who was ninety, and could remember back almost to the beginning of the century. Her memory was as clear as a bell, far better than Marge's. Her mother had to write everything down in lists or on the calendar on the back of the kitchen door. Even then she forgot things. Like coming to Alice's Parents' Day.

Then there was old Mr Gibbon whom Alice went in to see regularly. He'd been born and brought up in Surinam and had travelled all over the Far East, properly travelled in small boats, not on holiday packages, splashing about in turquoise-blue pools, eating burgers and hot dogs, sealed off from the local people. That was the way Alice meant to travel. Mr Gibbon had a fantastic agate collection. He said he'd leave it to her in his will; he knew she'd appreciate it. His nieces might just throw it in the bin. Mrs Moon and Mr Gibbon were far more interesting to talk to than Carol or Helen or Shona.

Alice took out her journal, recorded first the acquisition of her two new stamps. Then: 'Lizzie phoned. She seems to be liking her new life. Though she'd say she was, wouldn't she? She wouldn't let on if she wasn't. But she did sound keen. Her voice was all excited and kind of breathless, as if she was on a high. She said she loved her new room, that it's even better than this one. (Not that I care about that.) It's bigger, apparently. Painted pale grey and white with "touches of orange to relieve it," as she put it. (Very interior-designerish.) And better furnished. Well, you'd expect that, wouldn't you, him and her both being IDs. Lizzie said they'd set the room up really nicely for her, put flowers (roses, orange-coloured, with a "heavenly scent" – how does she know what heaven smells like?) in a vase beside her bed. And she's got a settee and a kettle. It sounds like a bed-sit.'

SIX

*U*sually Lizzie slept late on Sundays and had to be bullied out of bed by repeated calls and threats from her mother. But today she woke early and jumped up at once. She flung back the window and leant on the sill to look out at the garden. She loved it already, the way it was secluded, sheltered by tall beech trees. Mark had said that in autumn they looked like the colour of her hair!

A light mist was filming the smooth green lawn and shrouding the rose bushes, but even as she watched it began to lift. It was going to be another fine day.

It was so peaceful. So different from back home. She couldn't *help* thinking that. You couldn't walk up *that* garden without falling over something and twisting your ankle. And there was always washing on the drying green, day and night. Marge forgot to take it in half the time even when it was dry. (Candice had a dryer.) The flower borders grew in riotous profusion, the flowers too long and leggy for their own good, and Alice's vegetables sprouted in all directions.

Whenever she could get away with it she dug up another patch of grass.

'This is life!' That's what Marge would say. But *this* was, too. Why shouldn't life be peaceful and organised? It was just as 'real'. That was one of the words Marge and her friends used a lot. They used it to excuse their own chaos, thought Lizzie, pleased by her own flash of perception.

She thought about the previous afternoon. When she'd arrived with Mark, his wife and child had been waiting for them in the garden. She'd hung back a moment and looked at them sitting there on the white chairs against the green grass. They'd made a pretty picture. Lizzie had been conscious that they *were* his wife and child. They looked as if they belonged, whereas she was a visitor.

'Welcome,' said Candice, rising to meet her, though her voice was not quite as warm and welcoming as Lizzie would later report to Alice. There was a bit of stiffness in her embrace. But then, Lizzie felt stiff, too. And Cressida, when told to say hello, muttered inaudibly and looked sulky, which was also only to be expected. She was bound to feel a little jealous. She was an only child, used to all the attention. Peter had warned Lizzie that she'd have to make allowances in the beginning. Being a step-parent wasn't always easy, he'd said with a grin. 'There are bound to be overtones.'

Overtones, thought Lizzie, as she perched on a chair, sipping iced lemonade. They were talking politely, she and Candice, about trains, and how often

35

they ran to time, or didn't, and about the summer, how it had been very good so far, but no doubt underneath they were both thinking other thoughts.

It became easier once she'd been shown her room and had unpacked. When she came down afterwards, Mark said they were going to have a barbecue. 'On the terrace. Just the four of us. How does that strike you?'

'Lovely.'

The round white table was set with gleaming cutlery and shining glasses and prettily folded emerald-green paper serviettes. In the centre nestled a small bowl of peach-coloured rosebuds.

Mark was cook. He barbecued salmon steaks (in little aluminium foil parcels, with lemon and dill, which made Lizzie think of Alice), with potatoes also done on the grill, and a big crispy fresh salad, followed by strawberries and cream and Belgian chocolates. Lizzie was allowed two glasses of delicious white wine, but they didn't use the word 'allowed', as Marge would have done, meaning, 'Don't dare ask for any more!' Mark just poured it. He was really very understanding, thought Lizzie. And Candice was being terribly nice to her.

They'd sat until the sun went down, and they talked and talked. After a bit Cressida's head drooped and her eyes closed. Mark and Candice told Lizzie about their travels. They'd been all over the world, had gone to Australia and Hong Kong last year.

'It sounds wonderful,' sighed Lizzie, wishing the evening could last for ever.

But there would be other evenings. She saw them

stretching ahead, like shining pearls on a string, each one round and complete in itself.

The door bursting open broke her reverie. Cressy came marching into the room.

'There you are! What are you looking at in the garden?' She put her head out. 'I can't see anything. I'm starving. Can you give me my breakfast? They always sleep in on a Sunday.'

Cressy sat at the breakfast bar swinging her legs while Lizzie moved quietly round the black and white kitchen. She felt like being quiet, had no desire at all to raise her voice or shout at anybody. There was no need.

She set out fresh orange juice, muesli, peaches and bananas. Cressy chattered while they ate. Lizzie only half listened. Her head felt dreamy, as if she was still suspended between night and morning.

Mark came down around eleven in his dressing-gown to make a pot of coffee which he took back upstairs, along with a jug of orange juice, a couple of croissants, a bowl of strawberries and the Sunday papers.

'You girls all right?' he asked.

'Fine,' said Lizzie.

'I like having a sister,' said Cressy.

'I thought you would. It's nice to see the two of you getting along so well.' He smiled at them both, went out whistling.

Last night, before they'd left the terrace and the garden had become quite dark, he'd taken Lizzie aside and said, 'I've got the feeling you're going to fit in here.' The words had filled her with a warm glow.

'What shall we do today?' asked Cressy.

'I don't know. I hadn't thought.'

'We could play *Snakes and Ladders*.'

Lizzie hated – no, detested – *Snakes and Ladders*. It was so boring. It was one thing she and Alice were agreed upon. Alice had smuggled the family's board into the backyard one day and buried it in the bucket.

Cressy adored *Snakes and Ladders*. She crowed with glee when she went sailing up the ladders though her lip drooped when she had to come skidding down a snake. Lizzie allowed her to have several extra turns. She listened for sounds overhead while she rattled the dice in its cup. They must be reading every single page of every newspaper, including the ads.

It was well after noon before Candice appeared downstairs, dressed in ice-blue linen shorts and a white top. She was flapping her fingers about. She had newly painted the nails sherbet orange, and her toenails to match. Her arms and legs were smooth and brown, observed Lizzie, who felt like a ghost in comparison. Candice said she had a tan most of the year round, from travelling. Lizzie had freckles to go with her dark red hair and never tanned. She didn't even try to. Her mother had always been adamant about it. 'Want to get wrinkled skin when you're older? Skin cancer?'

'We're having a dinner party tonight,' said Candice. 'Just a few good friends. Mark will barbecue steaks and we'll have three or four salads with it. All nice and simple.'

'Can I give you a hand?'

'If you'd like to. Any good at cutting and chopping?'

Lizzie cut and chopped and took great care to do it neatly, while Candice arranged the salads in bowls, covering them with cling foil and putting them in the fridge when each was ready. Then they made small savouries for starters. While they worked they chatted, about clothes mostly, and Candice asked Lizzie if she had a boyfriend.

'No one steady,' she said.

'I've got a deep pink tee-shirt that would look great with your hair,' said Candice, and went to fetch it. She held it against Lizzie. 'Perfect! And we're more or less the same size.'

'Are you sure?'

'Absolutely. By the way, I wouldn't wear that purple tee-shirt again if I were you. It's too harsh a colour for your skin. You don't mind me telling you, do you?'

'Not at all,' said Lizzie, though she did, slightly, but she accepted the remark meekly. If it had been her mother who had made it she would have worn the tee-shirt defiantly for the rest of the day. But then Candice was not her mother. Only her step. And not a wicked or an unkind one.

She would wear the pink tee-shirt that evening, Lizzie decided, with her swirly green and pink skirt. Dinner parties! Evenings on the terrace! She must write to Carol and tell her all about her new life.

'Oh, by the way, Lizzie,' said Candice. 'I'm sure you must be wondering how I feel about you. It's not the easiest of situations, ours, so it's better that we acknowledge that. I just wanted you to know that I don't resent your existence! I mean to say, your mother was well before my time. Mark and I hadn't even met then.'

When they were having afternoon tea on the terrace, Candice remarked that there was a Punch and Judy show on in the park. 'At six.'

'Can I go?' clamoured Cressy. 'Please!'

'Better ask Lizzie if she'll take you.'

'Will you, Lizzie? *Please!*'

Mark laughed. 'You're going to have a job getting out of this one!'

Lizzie smiled. 'It's okay, Cressy, I'll take you.'

'And afterwards,' said Candice, 'I thought you might like to go to the ice-cream parlour opposite the park.'

'Can we go now?' Cressy leapt up.

'I don't see why not. You can always feed the ducks before the show. I'll put some bread in a bag for you.'

Candice gave Cressy the bag of bread to carry and tucked a folded twenty-pound note into Lizzie's hip pocket. 'For the show and the ice-cream. Have Knickerbocker Glories or Banana Splits or something special.'

The park was busy. Families were picnicking on the grass, playing ball games and flying kites. A line of small children edged the pond, flinging lumps of bread into the water with stiffly held arms. The ducks, satiated with too many offerings, swam snootily around in the middle of the water, displaying little interest.

'You throw, Lizzie,' begged Cressy. 'You've got longer arms.'

40

Lizzie tossed a couple of morsels after the others. 'I expect they'll eat it up later, when nobody's looking.'

They got seats in the front row for the Punch and Judy. They were early. Cressy jiggled around excitedly. Gradually the rows filled up, with children and parents. Lizzie saw that there was no one of her age amongst them.

The show was reasonably good and quite funny, although by the end Lizzie had had enough of puppets walloping one another over the head. She stifled a yawn when the children in the audience begged for an encore and the puppets obliged. She glanced at her watch. It was just gone seven. And they were supposed to go and eat ice-cream now – would *have* to – before returning home. She was anxious about the dinner party, didn't want to be late. What time had Candice said the guests were coming? Seven-thirty? Eight?

Punch and Judy took their last bow and a final swipe at one another before the curtain was tugged shut in front of them.

'That was great,' sighed Cressy. 'Who did you like best, Punch or Judy?'

'Probably Judy.'

'Me too. Wasn't it funny when she nipped his bottom and he shot up in the air?'

'Let's go,' said Lizzie. 'The time's getting on.'

The café was busy. They would have to wait for a table.

'Are you sure you want this ice-cream?' asked Lizzie.

'Sure,' said Cressy.

41

They stood in a line for twenty minutes before being seated.

Cressy studied the menu carefully, then decided on a Knickerbocker Glory, which was what she had said she'd have while they were queuing.

'What are you going to have?'

'Just a cappuccino. I don't want to spoil my dinner.'

Cressy ate her ice-cream slowly and with relish, Lizzie drank her coffee quickly and with increasing anxiety about the time.

'It doesn't matter when *we*'re back,' said Cressy.

It was ten past eight by the time they came up the front path. They could hear voices and laughter echoing from the terrace at the back.

Mark met them in the hall wearing a navy-blue and white striped apron. He had a glass in his hand.

'Sorry we're late,' said Lizzie.

'That's all right. We weren't worried. We knew Cressy was safe with you. Come on through to the terrace and meet the crowd.'

Three other couples were lounging around on the white chairs, drinking wine and eating the little savouries Candice and Lizzie had prepared earlier. They all looked as if they had just returned from the Caribbean. They greeted Cressy with whoops of delight. 'Gosh, you've shot up!' 'How pretty your hair's looking!' Cressy enjoyed the attention. She called them Uncle This and Aunt That. She slid on to obliging laps. Lizzie stood to one side feeling shy and awkward.

'And this is Lizzie.' Mark brought her forward. There was a chorus of 'Hi, Lizzie!'s. Did they know who she *really* was? Would he have told them? She supposed he must have done. But they didn't look like the kind of people to be bothered about that. They looked as if they'd take everything in their stride.

The barbecue was glowing red.

'Time to put the meat on, Mark,' said Candice, who was looking beautiful in a sleeveless coral-coloured dress to match her fingernails.

'Okay, I'll get the girls' burgers on first. Want to come and give me a hand, Lizzie?'

Lizzie followed him into the kitchen.

'If you'd just like to set trays for Cressy and yourself, put some salad on and so forth, I'll see to your meat. Would you like cheese or plain?'

Lizzie looked over at the side counter where the steaks were set out, peppered and ready for the grill. Eight steaks.

'Plain,' she said dully, feeling plain herself, and thinking of the pink tee-shirt and the sparkly earrings she'd planned to put on.

'I thought you and Cressy might like to eat in your room, have a picnic together.'

'I'd like a picnic,' said Cressy, who had come romping in.

She helped carry the trays upstairs.

'We'll set your table nicely, shall we, Lizzie? I'll ask Mummy if we can have a candle.'

My room will smell of burgers all night, thought Lizzie.

She left the window wide open. They could hear the guests below.

'Here we are then, kids,' cried Mark gaily, as he came sideways into the room carrying a large tray.

'I've done you two burgers each and Candice has made you some oven chips. Those are the only chips she'll have in the house, Lizzie. They don't smell the way ordinary ones do. Oh, and here's the tomato ketchup. Cressy loves tomato ketchup, don't you, Cress? And some Coke! Mustn't forget the Coke for you girls. Okay now? Got everything you need? Can you get your own desserts later? And bed at half past nine, Cressy, no later! That's far too late as it is. I expect Lizzie will read you a story, if you ask her nicely.'

'I like my daddy,' said Cressy as she upended the tomato sauce bottle and the ketchup glugged out on to her burger, almost swamping it. 'They don't always let me have ketchup. Just for treats. When they're having a party themselves. Then they say they'll let me have some if I'll be a good girl. That means they don't want me to bother them. Do you like my daddy?'

'Yes.'

Cressy chewed for a moment.

'How can he be your daddy too? He says he is. But he's not your *real* daddy, is he? It's just like I have Auntie Jill and Uncle Brian, isn't it? I just call them that. My daddy wasn't married to your mummy, was he?'

'Not exactly. Sort of.'

A burst of laughter erupted below and Lizzie resisted the impulse to get up and look down. To see them enjoying themselves. Of course they wouldn't want her at their party. She was only fifteen, and they were grown up, thirty – double her age – and even older.

She was just being silly. She'd have been the odd one out. She swallowed the last bit of her burger with difficulty, couldn't manage a second.

She took their dirty dishes downstairs and stacked them in the washer. Neither she nor Cressy felt like dessert. She went back up to her room to find the child sitting on her bed with a book on her knee.

'I want *Alice in Wonderland*.'

'My sister's called Alice.'

'Why are you looking like that?'

'Like what?'

'Sort of funny. Crumply.'

'I'm not at all crumply! Let's have the book, then. Move over!'

'Do you like living here?'

'Yes. Of course.'

'Do you like your room? It's not as pretty as mine, is it?'

'Oh, I don't know. It's just different. Mark and Candice fixed it up very nicely for me. It was kind of them.'

'Oh, they didn't fix it up specially for you. It used to be the au pair's.'

SEVEN

Alice didn't walk on the cracks on the pavement. A lot of people didn't, so she didn't feel odd. She walked to the shop, stepping neatly over the cracks, carrying Lizzie's letter in her pocket. She thought about the letter the whole way and the moment she opened the shop door she said to Mrs Kelly, who was leaning on the counter between the Kit-Kats and the Polo mints,

'Lizzie's living in the lap of luxury.' Marge, on tipping up the cornflake packet that morning to find it empty, had said, 'It's all right for Lizzie, living in the lap.' Alice had been in the middle of reading out the letter to her.

'She won't be in a hurry to get back here, then,' said Mrs Kelly.

'They have a dishwasher and a woman comes in every morning to clean. She's called Mrs Allison. She comes in her own car.'

'It's all right for some. Wish I didn't have to stand waiting for a bus in the morning. My corns are crucifying me something awful at present.'

'You shouldn't wear those shoes.' Alice pulled out the letter and polished her glasses. She read aloud, '"Mrs Allison does all the laundry, though I usually do my own ironing."' Alice looked up. 'Usually! Get that! You'd think she'd lived there for ever, instead of a week.'

'Sounds like the life of Riley. Eating salmon, drinking wine, sunning herself on the terrace!'

'Who was Riley?' asked Alice.

'Haven't a clue.'

'Must have been someone who knew how to live it up, anyway.'

'How's your mother?' Mrs Kelly's tone changed.

'She's not sick, you know. People keep asking about her as if she had rabies.'

'It's quite a thing, though, when your daughter ups and leaves, especially when it's —'

'The *Radio Times* have just come in.' Peter came through from the back. He was a bit grumpy this morning, had been since Lizzie's letter arrived. 'They need putting out.'

Mrs Kelly clattered off on her heels to the back shop.

Peter dumped a pile of women's magazines on the counter in front of Alice. 'I thought you were meant to be giving a hand for your 50p an hour? You might put these out on the stand.'

Alice folded up the letter and forbore to say anything about 50p an hour. She'd already said it. Slave labour! He couldn't afford to pay her any more, he'd retaliated. Take it or leave it. He wasn't supposed to employ her anyway, she was too young.

She arranged the glossy magazines on the rack. She didn't know any women who looked like the ones on the covers, with lips, teeth and hair all shining, and not a puff of wind ever to ruffle them. Candy Floss might, she supposed. She was tempted to draw a moustache on one of the languid, supercilious-looking models but her father wouldn't think that much of a joke.

She turned as the door blew open, and in came Zac back from his paper round. His tee-shirt was stuck to his chest. He always cycled as if the hounds of hell were yapping at his ankles, with his head down and his eyes glued to the road on either side of his spokes.

'Morning, Zachary,' said Alice.

He grunted, ducked his head to one side and tugged the paper sack over his head. As he did so the sack swung wide and swept the magazines off the rack that Alice had just arranged.

'Now look what you've done!'

'Sorry.'

'Fat lot of use that is. You could help pick them up. No, don't bother! You might mangle them even more. You've dented some of the glossy corners as it is. Better not let Peter see – he might give you the sack.'

'I've got it already.' Zac grinned and held up the bag.

'Ha, ha. Two out of ten!'

She put the dented magazines to the back.

'Guess who I heard from this morning?'

'Oh.' Zac tried to sound uninterested. 'How're things going?'

'Life is one long holiday. She just adores her father.'
Alice kept an eye on the back shop, for Peter's return.
He'd gone to answer the telephone. 'And she gets on a
dream with Candy Floss and Mustard Face.'

'Candy —?'

'Her step. Candice. And her half-sister, dearest
Cressida. Mustard and Cress. I'm calling her Mustard
Face for short.'

'That's not very short.'

'Don't be so irritating! You can be, you know.'

'So can you.'

'Okay, pax.'

'What does Lizzie do all day? She can't just sit
mooning at the roses, can she?'

'She swans around. She's been going swimming
every day – hey, get the pun? Not brilliant, I admit. They
belong to a sports club of course, Markie and Candy
Floss, no nasty, germy public pool for them, ponging
of chlorine. You might get verrucas there. Yuck!'

'Alice!' called Peter. 'You could put the kettle on
and make us all a cup of tea instead of standing out
there yacking.'

'Okay, Dad. Can we have Kit-Kats?'

'What do you think I am – made of money?'

Alice went through to the back shop followed by
Zac, and Mrs Kelly and her father took up their
positions behind the counter. A couple of workmen
who were digging up the road outside had come in.
The road was always being dug up, by the gas, the
electricity, cable TV. This was not a quiet corner. The
men would be wanting to buy cigarettes. Alice's father
didn't allow her to sell cigarettes.

She ran water into the kettle and Zac perched on the step-ladder.

'Mind yourself!' she warned. The ladder was wobbling.

Zac put one foot on the ground.

'You're not forgetting about the stamp fair, are you?' asked Alice. 'That's what I'm slaving my fingers to the bone for.'

After they'd had their tea (and Kit-Kats) and Zac had gone home, Alice got to thinking of ways of acquiring stamps without paying for them. There must be loads around that nobody wanted, that ended up in the rubbish bin. People who had friends and relatives abroad, for example. Now that was an idea! One she should have thought of before.

On her way home at lunch-time Alice stopped off at the Pakistani grocer on the corner. Her mother had asked her to buy milk. Khalil, the grocer's son, served her. He was in her class at school.

'I'm helping my dad out too,' she told him.

'It's something to do in the holidays.'

'Don't you like holidays?'

'They're all right. Get a bit bored sometimes.'

'Do you ever go to Pakistan?'

He shook his head. 'The fare costs a bomb.'

'And bombs are expensive. I expect you've got lots of relatives over there, though?'

'Lots.' He sounded gloomy. They probably had to send money back to support them. Just as well Marge and Peter didn't have to send money to anybody. It took them all they had to stay afloat.

'Do they write to your mum and dad?'

'Now and then.'

'Ah,' said Alice, and leaning in closer to the counter explained her interest in letters from abroad.

'No sweat,' said Khalil. 'Next time a letter comes I'll keep you the stamps.'

'Would you? That'd be fantastic!'

Out on the street, she wondered, where next? The chipper of course! She hurried along and as she neared it and smelled the smell she knew she was going to have to buy a bag of chips even though her mother wouldn't be pleased. She lathered them with salt and vinegar and brown sauce.

'Mr Barolli,' she said, putting a hot sizzly chip into her mouth, 'you came from Italy originally, didn't you?'

'Well, of course! Where else? Toscana! Tuscany. A beautiful region, of mountains and old villages. And ancient towns. Lucca. Siena.' His eyes grew damp. He began to reminisce. Alice found this interesting and would have liked to have heard more, but she didn't have time right now. She came to the point of her visit.

Mr Barolli promised he would save her all the stamps ever to come his way in the future. 'For a signorina like you, it will be a pleasure.'

He was full of blarney, was Mr Barolli, thought Alice as she hurried along the road, but nice with it. Blarney! Mr O'Friel in their street was Irish. From Dublin. Now why hadn't she thought of that before? She'd been dozing. And then there was the Thai restaurant just round the corner from where she was now. She took a detour to pass it, but it was closed. It mustn't open for lunch. She'd come back later. And there were two Chinese restaurants on the main road. And an Indian only half a mile away. She felt as if she'd struck a deep golden seam and all she had to do was mine it.

'Where have you been?' asked her mother when she came in. 'I've been waiting for the milk. I want to make macaroni cheese.' She sniffed. 'You've been in the chip shop, haven't you?'

'You'd think I'd been taking drugs. There's nothing wrong with chips. Potatoes are good for you. They're full of nutrition.'

'You can eat better at home, that's all. And who knows what kind of fat they cook them in.'

Alice made no reply for her mother was not consistent. When she was in the right mood she'd send them for carry-outs to the Chinese and Indian and even the chipper and she didn't bother her head two hoots what the stuff was cooked in then.

'I want chips for my dinner,' Jamie wailed.

'Now look what you've started!' said Alice's mother.

Alice went upstairs and washed her hands (she didn't like the lingering chip smell, either) and took up her journal to make a quick entry.

'Had a letter from Frizzie Lizzie today, full of the joys. Can they be true? Sounds too good to me. Or am I being a jealous green-eyed monster, ha, ha? Don't think it would suit me, that life, from the sound of it. All those people with golden tans laughing on the terrace. Wouldn't mind the money, though. Then

I could buy all the stamps I wanted. Hey, Markie and Candy Floss! They travel the world. They go to foreign parts. I'll write to Lizzie tonight. Might as well milk them for something.'

EIGHT

'*I*s that a letter from your sister?' asked Cressy. 'Your real sister?'

'You're my real sister, too.'

Cressy was still not convinced about that.

'But, yes, it is, it's a letter from Alice.'

'What does she say?'

'Oh, all sorts of things, about herself and the family and Zac.'

'That's a funny name.'

'Some people think he's a funny boy.'

'Do you?'

Lizzie shrugged. 'I'm used to him.'

'Is he Alice's boyfriend?'

'She's too young to have a boyfriend. She's only eleven.'

'I've got a boyfriend and I'm only seven. He's called Philip and he sits next to me in class. He lets me use his Winnie the Pooh rubber.'

'Well, Zac is too old for Alice. He's my age. And Alice, although she's old for her age in some ways, is young in others.'

'What ways?'

'Never mind.' Lizzie often found herself starting to say something to Cressy and then drawing herself up when she remembered she was only seven. She folded the letter and stuffed it back in its envelope.

'You're looking sort of funny again,' said Cressy, spooning up the last of her cereal.

Lizzie felt funny. She had that ache at the back of her throat again. She fingered her neck. Could she have a cold coming on? It didn't seem the right time of year for colds, the weather had continued to be warm and sunny. She supposed she was feeling a bit – well, okay then – homesick. Now that she'd admitted it, it came over her in a rush, and she thought she might even be coming down with flu. It felt like something physical. But it was only natural, though, wasn't it, to be homesick when you first went away from home? It would pass. Like the flu. You just had to stick it out. Her friend Carol's sister had been miserable for the whole of the first term she was away at university. She'd cried every night, so her mother had told Marge, and then, at the start of the next term she was as happy as anything, and now wild horses wouldn't drag her home.

'So don't worry, Alice,' Lizzie told her sister inside her head, 'I won't be coming back to take my room away from you. I'm settling down here really very nicely. There's bound to be the odd blip now and then.'

She found that she chatted quite regularly to Alice, especially when she went to bed at night and wanted to talk down the day. Alice was the only other person she had to talk to for most of the day, apart from Cressy, and Mrs Allison in the mornings. Mark and Candice left the house for work at eight sharp every morning, just as she and Cressy were getting up. Lizzie usually tried to get up a few minutes earlier so that she could spend them in the kitchen alone with her father. But he didn't have much time then of course. He'd be swallowing his coffee, taking a quick glance at the *Financial Times* and Candice would be calling to him, 'Ten to eight, darling. Five to. Have you got that file for the Manson job?' 'Must rush, Lizzie,' he'd say and get up, giving her a quick kiss on the top of her head. It was worth getting up early for that kiss. And just to see him.

'Are we going swimming this morning?' asked Cressy.

'I expect so.'

They heard feet on the back door scraper and then Mrs Allison came in.

'Morning, girls! How are we this morning, then? It's another lovely morning. Can't believe our luck. A good summer at last!'

Cressy went upstairs to change into her shorts and fetch her swimming costume. Lizzie cleared the breakfast dishes from the table.

'See your dad this morning?' asked Mrs Allison, pulling on her yellow rubber gloves.

Mrs Allison was an awful gossip but Lizzie couldn't resist talking to her. Especially about her dad. She'd talk to anyone about her dad.

'We had breakfast together. Well, coffee, at any rate.'

'They work hard, those two,' commented Mrs Allison. 'Ambitious. Noses to the grindstone. Nothing wrong with that. Better than being lazy, I say. I've never been one to sit on my rear-end myself.'

'They're often not back till seven at night. Some-times later.'

'Don't suppose she cooks then?'

'I make something for myself and Cressy earlier. They just have an omelette or maybe a meal from the freezer. If they're quite late they have a bite to eat on the way home.' They'd done that last night. Mark had rung at seven and said, 'We'll be late, Lizzie. Don't wait up.' She'd heard them coming in at eleven.

'Not much home life.'

'They're at home all week-end. They spend a lot of time in the garden.'

'Entertain a lot.' Mrs Allison got the cleaning up to do next morning. Still, as she said, that was what she was here for.

'They've got tons of friends.'

'Seem to have more time for them than their own child.'

'Cressy's perfectly happy,' said Lizzie defensively, not sure that that was true.

'Are you happy, then? Being here? Get on well with your dad?'

'Oh, yes, very well! I can't imagine a hard word between us or quarrelling or anything like that.' Lizzie laughed at the very idea.

'He's a charmer, I've got to hand it to him.' Mrs Allison glanced sideways at Lizzie. 'And how do you find her?'

'She's been very nice to me, I can't complain at all. She's been giving me clothes and make-up and bits and pieces of jewellery.'

'The last au pair girl that was here didn't get on with her.'

'No?'

'Mrs Wheeler was jealous of her. Oh, yes.' Mrs Allison lowered her voice. 'There was a big row. I shouldn't be talking to you like this, of course.'

'That's all right,' said Lizzie uncertainly.

'Lizzie!' yelled Cressy from above.

'What is it?' Lizzie went to the door.

'I can't find my yellow bikini. The one with the Mickey Mouses on.'

'Look in your bottom drawer.'

'Can't you look?'

'No, I'm busy.' Lizzie closed the door.

'You're quite right,' said Mrs Allison. 'Put her in her place once in a while. She can be a bit of a little madam wanting this and wanting that.'

Lizzie moved up to the draining board and parked herself close to Mrs Allison. She cleared her throat. 'You were saying . . .'

'Oh, about the au pair girl?' Mrs Allison squirted cleanser into the sink and attacked the stainless steel. 'She was a lovely girl. A real stunner. Italian. Big dark eyes and beautiful thick dark hair. You know the type? Really sexy way of talking. Just came natural to her, I suppose. It does for some of these foreigners.' Mrs Allison rinsed out her cloth and hung it over the tap. 'She was called Donatella. Your dad used to make a point of chatting to her.'

'Candice didn't like that?'

'Oh no! You can bet your sweet life she didn't! She likes undivided attention, haven't you found? Ended up with an unholy row. I was here. They didn't go to work that morning. For once business took second place. He said he was only being nice to Donatella, making her feel welcome.'

'I'm sure that was true,' said Lizzie hotly.

'You could be right. But she wasn't having any. "She's got to go!" she said. "Today! I don't want her under my roof another minute and you can be the one to tell her!"'

'Poor Dad.'

'It had happened before. There's been a string. From France, Spain, Denmark, all over. "I'm finished with au pairs!" she said. "That's it! We'll have to make alternative arrangements."'

'I see,' said Lizzie. She fiddled with the soap dish. 'When did all this happen?'

'Couple of weeks before you came.'

The door opened behind them, making Lizzie jump guiltily. Cressy stood there with a drooping lip.

'I can't find my bikini and you won't even come and help. I'm going to tell my mummy on you!'

'Now, now, temper tantrums!' remonstrated Mrs Allison. 'If you ask me nicely maybe *I* can find it for you.' She dried her hands. 'Well, I'm waiting.'

'Don't want to ask nicely.'

'That's all right then. Do without. And I don't mind if you tell your mummy. You see, your mummy needs me. Calls me her treasure, she does.'

'Please, Mrs Allison, can you find my bikini?' asked Cressy sulkily.

'That's better. If you come with me into the laundry room perhaps you'll be lucky.' Mrs Allison looked back at Lizzie. 'You see, it's just a matter of being firm with them.'

NINE

'There's a letter for you,' said Marge, when Alice came in at lunch-time, late again. She'd been doing a stamp trawl on her way home and had quite a big catch in her carrier bag. Her mother and Johnny were already at the table and Jamie was in his high chair. Peter didn't come home for lunch, he ate a sandwich in the back shop.

A bulky-looking envelope was lying on the table at Alice's place.

'Why does she never write to me?' asked Marge.

'You don't write to her.'

'I did. I sent her a card.' Marge sighed. She'd been sighing a lot since Lizzie had gone and talking about failure, instead of celebrating the liberation she'd been waiting for. 'I feel there's such a gap between us.'

'There is,' said Alice, sitting down and taking up the envelope. 'A hundred miles.'

Her mother gave her a look intended to squash and turned her attention to Jamie who was shouting, 'More, more!'

Alice slit open the envelope and tipped it upside down. Out came a flurry of postage stamps.

'Can I have some?' demanded Johnny, making to grab one.

'Certainly not!' Alice elbowed his hand away.

She spread them in front of her on the table. 'Thailand. Italy. Hong Kong! Australia. New Zealand. I knew they went to loads of foreign parts.'

'Eat your lunch before it gets cold,' said her mother. 'Probably is already. What were you doing anyway to make yourself late? Pestering people, I suppose.'

Alice did not reply, she was too busy examining her new acquisitions. She was going to have a busy afternoon soaking them all off their backings. She helped herself to shepherd's pie. It was not overly warm but she'd better not complain about that.

'Aren't you going to read your letter?' asked her mother.

'You told me to eat my lunch.'

'No doubt you're capable of doing both at the same time.'

Alice unfolded the letter. Four pages.

'Not like Lizzie to write such long letters,' commented her mother. 'What's the news, then?'

'Give me a minute,' grumbled Alice, scanning the first page quickly. 'It's all much as before. Markie and Candy Floss are working terribly hard . . .'

'Candy Floss!' Marge laughed. 'I must say I thought she looked a bit like it in the photographs. And I bet he wouldn't like to be called Markie. Go on, what else?'

'Mrs Allison is *wonderful* to talk to. So sympathetic.'

Marge's smile faded. 'She'll talk to the cleaning lady, but not to her own mother!'

'Give it a rest, Mum, ' Alice wanted to say, but no doubt she'd get clouted for being cheeky. If Peter were here that's what he'd tell Marge and she'd subside and admit, 'Okay, I know I shouldn't go on.' Alice found it annoying that there should be different rules for children and adults.

'This looks more interesting,' she said, rustling the letter. "We went to the sports club yesterday, as usual, to swim, and we were sitting in the Jacuzzi afterwards when I got talking to a girl and a couple of boys about my own age. They're called Pam and Simon and Richard. Pam is super. I got on with her straight away. She's going out with Simon. I have to say that I thought Richard was pretty fab!!!' Alice looked up. 'Three exclamations marks.'

'Trust Lizzie!' said Marge. 'I didn't think it would take her long to make friends. Put her on the moon and she'd find the nearest spaceman.'

'What's excam-nation marks?' asked Johnny.

'It means, now look here, pay attention, this is important,' said Alice. She read on. '"Afterwards we went to the café and drank Coke."'

'Wonder where Cressy was,' interrupted Marge.

'With them, I expect. She'd have been lugged along. Now where was I? Oh yes. "They've asked me to join them for tennis tomorrow, to make up a four-some. Candice is going to lend me a tennis dress, which is very nice of her. It's pretty swish, with little hand–embroidered blue flowers around the neck and hem. She's lending me a racket, too. I was wishing I'd

63

brought mine but it's just as well I didn't. It's not up to much and one of the strings has gone. You can have it if you want, but then I don't suppose you do. You can give it to Johnny to play with in the garden."'

'I like that!' said Marge, clearly not liking it. 'We gave her that racket just two years ago for her birthday. Nothing will be good enough for madam now.'

'Do you want to hear the rest?' demanded Alice. '"In case you're wondering what Richard looks like – and knowing how nosy you are, you will – I'd better tell you. He's tall and dark and very good-looking and he's got a nice smile."' Alice folded the letter. 'Sounds like Markie.'

'Mm,' said her mother thoughtfully. 'I was just thinking that myself.'

After she'd washed the dishes Alice went upstairs to begin her stamp-soaking operation. First, she filled the wash hand basin with water and then she floated the stamps on top. It was a job to get them all in. She'd picked up quite a number, from Mr Barolli (along with another little chat on Tuscany), one of the Chinese restaurants, a customer at the shop who had relatives in half the states of the U.S.A., and Mr O'Friel in the street. She was to go back and see Khalil later. Then there were the offerings from Markie and Candy Floss.

She regarded her little flotilla with satisfaction. People were only too pleased to save stamps for her; they didn't feel she was pestering them in the slightest. The woman with the American relatives had said

64

she'd wished she'd known Alice was interested, she'd thrown thousands in the bin.

When the stamps had soaked for long enough Alice lifted them out, one by one, and carefully eased off the backing. Then she placed them neatly all around the edge of the bath to dry.

Her mother poked her head in. 'I'm just taking the kids to the swing park.' She saw the stamps. 'Are you going to leave that lot there?'

'Just for a couple of hours. Just till they're dry. This is educational, Mum. I'm studying the countries of the world.'

'You should be outside in the fresh air.'

'Playing rounders. Yes, I know.'

'Don't blame me if Johnny touches them.'

'He'll be at the swing park, won't he?'

Her mother departed.

Alice let the water out of the sink and gathered up the torn soggy bits of envelope. Why couldn't parents let you be? Why were they were always trying to turn you into something else? Swans into ducks. Ducks into swans. Swans could be quite vicious creatures. Once, when she was little and in the park with Lizzie, a swan had chased them, honking and making a terrible racket. The sight of its beak and the glint in its eye had made her give swans a wide birth for ever after.

She went into her room and sat on the bed, reading Lizzie's letter through again. Lizzie did seem to be having rather a nice time. She didn't appear to be missing them at all. Of course she wouldn't say if she were, would she? But the chances were that she wasn't, not with Richard and Pam and Simon taking up her attention. As well as Mark. Alice looked up from the letter. Mr Murgatroyd next door was cutting his grass. The sound of the mower mingled with the shouts of children playing further down the terrace. Summery, out-of-door sounds. Dust motes danced in the shaft of sunshine beaming in through the open window.

She put the letter back in its envelope. Maybe she should go out and get a few whiffs of this fresh air that her mother was so keen on.

Alice drifted downstairs and out into the street. She looked up the way and down the way. No sign of Mr Gibbon in his garden; he'd probably be having an afternoon nap. As would Mrs Noon. Alice hovered on the edge of the pavement, tilting her toes down into the gutter, tipping the weight of her body forward. It was seldom that she felt uncertain about what to do. What was wrong with her today? It was Lizzie's letter, she supposed, so full of the joys. Lizzie's joys. Well, Lizzie had *gone*. And she'd just have to get used to that.

She gave herself a shake. She couldn't stand here all afternoon. She'd go along and see if Khalil was back.

As she neared his shop she saw three youths up ahead. Three troublemakers. With fat heads and tattoos on their arms. They sometimes came into their shop and once or twice had managed to grab something, a bottle of Coke, a few bars of chocolate, whatever came to their thieving hands. The cigarettes were out of their reach, behind the counter. Her dad tried to head them off when he saw them coming, bar the door and tell them to be off or he'd call the cops. Not that they were that easily frightened. On one occasion, when he did call them, they hung around until the policeman turned up and then said, 'We've not done nothing. We're just stood here. It's a free country innit? You're allowed to stand.' The next night, somebody chucked a rock through the window, and after that Peter had had to put wire mesh over the windows.

Alice slowed when she saw the boys. She saw them stop outside Khalil's shop, beside the trays of fruit and vegetables that were set out on the pavement. In the next instant orange balls were flying in all directions. The boys had upended a crate. Now they were moving off, jostling one another, and laughing.

'You think you're great,' muttered Alice. 'Pea-heads!'

Khalil had emerged from the shop waving his arms and shouting. She ran up to him and he dropped his shoulders in a gesture of resignation.

'Look at our oranges!' he said mournfully.

The pieces of fruit were rolling along the pavement and some had landed in the gutter. A couple had bounced into the middle of the road where they lay, skins burst open, the flesh splayed out. The wheels of a double decker bus had just passed over them.

'I'll help you pick them up,' said Alice.

They chased oranges together, pursuing them into nooks and crannies. Half of them would be unsaleable and would have to be dumped, said Khalil. They couldn't sell damaged fruit. 'You can take some home with you, if you'd like.'

'Can I?' asked Alice. 'My mum's got a juicer. She loves fresh orange juice. She's into vitamins in a big way.'

She set off back home with stamps from Pakistan in her pocket and a bag filled with burst oranges. The bag was so heavy she had to rest every few yards. She hadn't liked to ask Khalil for a second carrier to break up the load. Carriers cost money. She was glad enough to get the oranges. They should cheer Marge up. A bag of fruit for nothing! Marge was in need of cheering. She was forever going on these days about how hard it was to be a mother.

As Alice passed the tennis courts she heard the thud of balls and the call of voices. Another summery sound. After Wimbledon the courts were always busier. Four girls from her class were playing on the nearest court. One – Hilda – saw her through the wire while she was gathering up the balls and waved and shouted, 'Hi, Alice!'

'Hi!' Alice raised her free hand in return. She watched them for a moment, resting her shoulder. They weren't very good, they wouldn't make the tennis club finals, never mind Wimbledon. They kept swiping at the ball and missing it, coming in either too low or too high, but they were laughing a lot and chattering between serves. They seemed to be having a good time.

Alice picked up the bag and moved on. Lizzie was good at tennis, had won the under-fourteen girls sin- gles' title at the club two years ago. She might be out on a tennis court right at this very moment serving to tall, dark, handsome Richard.

TEN

'*I* don't want to go to the silly old tennis courts,' said Cressy.

Lizzie remembered Mrs Allison's advice about being firm. 'Well, you're going, whether you like it or not. And your mummy knows we're going. She's lent me her dress.' Lizzie let the pleated skirt swirl around her legs.

'My mummy looks nicer in it than you do.'

Lizzie felt her confidence plummet and was annoyed that it should. It was ridiculous to care what a child said, particularly a sulky child who'd had its nose put out of joint. Lizzie had spent the last hour upstairs getting dressed, had been in agony wondering whether she would look good enough for Pam and Simon, and of course Richard. And had been annoyed with herself for being so bothered. She remembered what her mother had said to her when she'd been going out on her first date. 'He's probably as nervous as you are.' But Richard hadn't looked the nervous type.

Lizzie knew what Alice would say. 'All that fuss for a boy! You're off the wall.'

'Get your sandals on, Cressy,' ordered Lizzie. 'Or else we'll be late.'

'It'll be boring at the tennis courts.'

Lizzie took the sandals out of Cressy's hands and knelt to put them on herself. Cressy bunched her feet up and made them as awkward as possible. Really, she was worse than Johnny at times and he was only four!

'Can I play tennis too?' asked Cressy. 'Can I get a turn?'

'Probably,' said Lizzie, thinking how easy it was to start lying to a child when you felt exasperated. And she felt quite exasperated. Ouch! She sucked her finger. She'd stabbed it on the sandal buckle. She fastened up the buckles quickly and got off her knees. There was a dirty mark on her skirt where Cressy's foot had rested. 'Damn! Right then, Cressy, let's get a move on!'

Before leaving Lizzie sponged the mark but that seemed only to make it worse, to spread it. Maybe they shouldn't go after all. She'd look such a tramp. She felt hot all over, and damp under the arms. But now Cressy was off dancing down the path bearing the racket aloft like a spear and shouting, 'Come on, Lizzie! Lazy Lizzie!'

Pam and Simon and Richard were waiting on the veranda of the clubhouse. They looked cool and re-laxed in their spotless white clothes.

'Sorry I'm late,' said Lizzie, pushing her damp hair back behind her ears.

'That's all right.' Richard gave her a nice smile.

'Our court's not due for ten minutes yet.' He glanced at Cressy, who beamed back at him.

'I hope you don't mind,' said Lizzie.

'No, that's okay.'

When it was time they strolled out to the court. Pam going in front with Simon, Lizzie walking behind with Richard, and Cressy. Cressy chattered like a sparrow on a high wire.

'I thought you and I would partner one another, Lizzie,' said Richard. 'That all right with you?'

'Oh yes, fine. Cressy's going to sit at the side, aren't you, Cressy?'

Cressy stood in the middle of the court with her legs planted wide apart. 'You said I could have a turn.'

'Maybe later.'

'I want it *now*. That's not fair! You promised.'

'I did not *promise*.' Lizzie leant over Cressy and lowered her voice. 'Get off the court, Cressy, and be a good girl. I'll buy you a Mars bar later.'

'That's bribery.'

Lizzie felt sweat trickling off her forehead. She saw Richard twirling his racket between his hands. Pam and Simon were leaning against the net post. They were wasting good playing time.

'Please, Cressy, get *off*! Or I shall become really angry, I warn you!'

'What would you do? You're not allowed to hit me.'

That was exactly what she felt like doing, Lizzie realised.

Richard intervened. 'Let's give her a couple of balls to hit and then you'll go and sit at the side, won't you, Cressy?'

Cressy returned his smile. 'Will you hit the balls to me, Richard?'

Lizzie seethed at the side of the court while Cressy messed around missing balls and shrieking with joy. She managed to touch only one with the racket, even though Richard was throwing the balls straight at the strings. Pam and Simon were trying to look amused, but Lizzie could see that they weren't really, not underneath.

'Do you have to mind the kid all the time?' asked Pam. 'Must be a bind.'

Lizzie was saved from answering by being struck on the back of the thigh with a ball.

'I think that'll do now, Cressy,' said Richard. 'It's our turn.'

'Oh,' wailed Cressy. '*Please*! I didn't get to hit it much.'

'Come on now.' Richard spoke decisively. He steered her off. 'You can be the ball girl, like they do at Wimbledon. Have you seen them on the telly? Squat over there at the side of the net and keep your eyes skinned.'

'Have you got younger brothers and sisters?' asked Lizzie, as she and Richard moved on to their half of the court.

'One of each.'

She felt greatly relieved. And his mother wasn't a widow. He'd made some reference to his father when they were in the clubhouse.

Lizzie was a better player than any of the others, that became evident once they got going. Peter had taught her when she was quite small. He'd been junior champion for his region when he was at school.

Cressy entered into her new role with enthusiasm, too much, for Lizzie's liking. For everyone's. She scurried madly across the court in pursuit of each ball, getting in the way and taking her time to deliver it, thus holding up the game. And when she was on Lizzie and Richard's side of the court she made sure to present the ball always to Richard.

Lizzie and Richard took the first set.

'You were brilliant,' he said, as they changed ends. 'That's a sizzler of a serve you've got.'

Lizzie flushed with pleasure.

'Will you be finished soon?' asked Cressy. 'I'm getting bored being a ball girl. I have to do all the running and you just walk about.'

Two games later, Cressy announced she needed the loo.

'There's one in the clubhouse,' said Pam, who was standing at the baseline, arm half raised, ready to serve.

'I'm not allowed to go to strange toilets on my own.'

'Just hang on a bit,' said Lizzie, squaring up to take the serve.

'I need now, shouted Cressy, just as Pam served. '*Now!*'

Lizzie missed the return. It was an easy return and she shouldn't have fluffed it. That damn child! She was jumping around on the sideline as if she was in agony. Which Lizzie doubted. But what if she had an accident? Really, Cressy was too old for all this carry on! She was not going to give in to her, she could jolly well wait!

But Lizzie's concentration was gone. She missed the next ball too. Pam and Simon won the game.

'Better take her to the loo,' advised Richard.

'Come on!' Lizzie glared at Cressy.

They walked over to the clubhouse. 'You should have gone before we left the house,' said Lizzie.

'I didn't need then.'

They found the Ladies and Cressy disappeared into a cubicle. She stayed there for ages. Lizzie ran her fingers through her hair and pouted at herself in the mirror. Her freckles seemed to be darkening, blast them! She paced the floor, arms folded.

'Cressy, are you all right?' she asked through the door.

'Yes.' The voice was muffled.

'You're not feeling sick or anything?'

'No.'

'Well, hurry up!'

It was another couple of minutes before the flush went. Cressy emerged and went to a basin to wash her hands. She lathered her hands with soap over and over again, and right up above the wrists.

'Get a move on!'

'I *am* moving! I have to wash my hands properly or else I'll get nasty germs. Mummy says.'

Lizzie couldn't take any more, she blew her lid. 'You're just doing this deliberately,' she shouted. 'To wreck my morning!'

Cressy let out a loud, high-pitched wail and began to cry.

The door opened, and in came two women wearing snow-white tennis dresses. They looked at Cressy and

74

then at Lizzie. Accusingly, Lizzie thought. Cressy was sobbing as if her heart was broken. Lizzie could do nothing other than comfort her.

'It's all right, Cressy. Don't cry, please don't cry.'

Cressy's shoulders gradually subsided and she allowed Lizzie to wipe her tear-stained face.

'Can we go for ice-cream after?' she asked.

'I expect so.'

'Promise!'

'Okay, I promise,' said Lizzie wearily.

As they came out of the clubhouse they saw Pam and Simon and Richard were leaving the court. Their time must be up.

'We thought we'd go to a coffee bar downtown,' said Richard. 'There's a new one just opened. It's all done out in green and white marble, I believe.'

'Sounds like the one our father designed.'

'Oh, really?' Richard was impressed. 'Want to come along?'

'I don't know if I can. You see, I promised Cressy I'd take her for ice-cream.'

'I expect you'll be able to get ice-cream there.'

'I don't want to go downtown,' said Cressy. 'I want to go to the ice-cream parlour opposite the park. That's where we always go. That's where my mummy says I have to go.'

'You don't have to go to just one place.' Lizzie tried to sound amused.

'Yes, I do.'

Richard turned to Lizzie. 'What about joining us later? We're going to see a film in the evening. Would you be free?'

'I think so. What time would it be?'

'Film starts at eight. We could meet up at half past seven.'

That should be all right, said Lizzie. They arranged a meeting place and it was agreed that if she wasn't there by twenty to eight she would see them at the cinema.

She thought about the evening all day, changed her mind several times about what she would wear. She washed her hair and blow dried it instead of letting it dry in the sun the way she usually did.

'Do you love Richard?' asked Cressy.

'Don't be silly! I hardly know him. You don't love people that easily.'

'Not even my daddy?'

Lizzie blushed, as if she had no right to love him. But she did have a right. He was her father, too.

She ate with Cressy at six o'clock and was dressed and ready to go by ten to seven.

'Read me a story,' begged Cressy.

'I can't, I'm going out in a minute. Your mummy and daddy will be in soon. They can read to you.'

'My mummy only ever reads for five minutes.'

Seven struck on the clock in the hall. Please don't be late tonight, Lizzie begged inside her head. She wouldn't be able to bear it if they were late. They'd been home at seven sharp the last two evenings. And if they were going to be late they usually rang before this.

At three minutes past seven the telephone began to shrill on the kitchen wall. Lizzie leapt to answer it.

'We're going to be a bit late, I'm afraid, Lizzie,' said Candice.

'But you can't!' cried Lizzie. 'I've got a date in half an hour with Richard, the boy I was playing tennis with. I've arranged to meet him.'

'You didn't say anything about that this morning. If you had we could have made other arrangements. We could have asked Mrs Allison to baby-sit.'

'I didn't know this morning.'

'Well, I'm sorry, Lizzie, but there's nothing we can do about it now. We're in the middle of an important meeting with clients and we can't just walk out. You understand that, don't you?'

'Well, yes, but —'

'This is our livelihood, Lizzie. We have to eat. All of us. You can go out some other evening.'

ELEVEN

'*T*hey're trying to socialise me,' Alice wrote in her journal. 'I have to go to Cheryl's birthday *party*. Yuck pooh! Can you imagine *me* at a party?'

Cheryl was the daughter of Marge's friend Ginny, the one that she sat in the kitchen with for hours talking about life, and lamenting the fact that Alice didn't have dozens of friends like other children of her age.

'Cheryl is twelve today,' continued Alice, writing in leisurely fashion with the fountain pen she'd been given for her own eleventh birthday. She loved writing with a fountain pen. The nib glided so smoothly over the paper. And the paper felt good under the nib. She liked good quality paper, hated the kind that let the ink show through on the other side. Lizzie called her a Fuss Pot.

'As if I could care less what age Cheryl is! And I'm sure she doesn't want me at her party any more than I want to go. Ginny will have given her a good talking to. "Now I want you to be nice to Alice, make her feel welcome. Her mother is my very best friend, we've known one another since we were at school." As if Cheryl wouldn't know all that already! But it seems that mothers have to go over and over the same thing until you'd think they'd bore themselves rigid. Whenever Ginny comes to visit she and Marge seem to have be having a rerun of the conversation they had the last time.'

'Alice,' called Marge from downstairs, 'are you nearly ready?'

'Yes.'

'You'll need to leave in ten minutes. You don't want to be late.'

'No?' murmured Alice.

She resumed writing. 'So here I am all dressed up like a sugar plum fairy! Marge dug out an old dress of Lizzie's. It's pale blue and has little cap sleeves and a full skirt. "I remember Lizzie going to Carol's party in this dress and she looked lovely," she said. I didn't make the obvious remark about not being Lizzie. I wish Lizzie *was* here! Well, for half an hour anyway. She'd have backed me up. She'd have told them not to make me go to something I didn't want to go to. She'd have said, "Let's go to the movies, kid sister." I don't know why I am going to this awful party. I'm sure it'll be putrid. Well, I suppose I do know. They went on and on at me, or at least Marge did, until she made me feel like a freak for not going to birthday parties. "Every other kid in the neighbourhood goes."'

'Alice!' called Marge again.

'I'm coming!'

Alice closed her journal and put it away in the bottom of her drawer, under a pile of socks and knickers. She made a face at herself in the mirror and went downstairs.

'You look fantastic,' said Marge brightly. Too brightly. 'Why don't you leave your glasses behind? You can see well enough without them, can't you?'

'No, not well enough. If I did I wouldn't wear them.'

'But just for the party?'

Alice held on to the legs of her spectacles with both hands. She absolutely refused to see the world through a blur for the sake of some rotten old party. Whether she would like it or not, she wanted to see what was going on.

'Don't forget your present,' said Marge.

Alice picked up the parcel, wrapped in glittering silver and blue paper with a silver rosette in the middle. Cheryl would know she hadn't wrapped it. Or bought it, either. It was an enormous bottle of rose-smelling bubble bath.

'Have a lovely time!' cried her mother gaily.

'Do you like sending lambs to the slaughter?' asked Alice.

'Think positively! If you expect to enjoy it you probably will. And remember that Dad will pick you up at ten o'clock.'

'I might want to come home before then. Like seven-thirty.' It was ten past seven now.

'You can give us a ring if you have to.'

Alice bared her teeth and set forth.

As she went down the path Zac was coming out of his front door.

'Where are you going? All dressed up like that?'

'You might well ask!'

He fell into step beside her and they walked along the road.

'If you must know, I'm going to Cheryl's birthday party.'

He groaned.

'You see! You wouldn't want to go, would you?' For one mad moment she had hoped he might, that she could have taken him along and they could have sat in a corner and talked about stamps or going to the moon or what it would be like to be trapped underground for three days. Anything but play *party games*.

They chatted on the corner for a few minutes and then Alice continued on round into the next street, where Cheryl lived. She took her time. She stopped to look in gardens, to stroke a marmalade cat draped along a wall. By now it was a quarter to eight. She heard the party din as she approached. You'd think they had a hundred and fifty in their front room instead of the twenty they'd said they were having.

The worst of the noise was coming from a music centre. Alice hated loud music. Lizzie had been forbidden to play her tranny too loudly, though when Marge and Peter went out she would turn it up and Alice would go in and scream at her and they'd have an argy-bargy. Alice would usually get it turned down a bit, at least.

Alice rang the bell, but didn't lean too hard, in the hope that it might not be heard. But it was. By Ginny, all decked out in a long gauzy orange dress and numerous bangles which slid up and down her arm when she waved her hands about. She waved her hands about all the time, couldn't say anything without doing it. Marge said that was how Ginny expressed herself.

'Alice!' cried Ginny, and the bangles rattled. 'We've been wondering where you were!'

You were, thought Alice. Not Cheryl. She'd be one of the ravers.

'As a matter of fact I'd just rung your mother to see if you were coming. Maybe you'd better call her back. She said you left ages ago.'

'Hardly ages. She always exaggerates. But I suppose she'll be thinking I've been abducted.'

Alice rang from the wall phone in the kitchen. 'I'm here. All in one piece. Nobody tried to snatch me. Unfortunately.' She replaced the receiver.

'I love your sense of humour, Alice,' said Ginny.

The kitchen walls were vibrating.

'Hope the neighbours don't mind loud music,' Alice said – shouted – to Ginny. There was no sign of Cheryl's dad. He was probably in the pub playing dominoes. Wise man.

'I warned them.' Ginny grinned. 'Bribed them, too. Bottle of wine apiece. They've gone out for the evening.'

'Can I give you a hand?' Alice looked round the kitchen.

'Nothing to do. We're just having nibbles, little sausage rolls, things like that, and pizza – I've made heaps, with all sorts of interesting toppings – and there's juice and Coke. No, you go on through and enjoy yourself, Alice. That's what you're here for! Let me take you in.'

Ginny led the way.

'Cheryl!' she yelled from the doorway. She had to advance halfway into the room to make herself heard. 'Come and say hello to Alice!'

Cheryl was dancing with one of her friends. They were gyrating madly and rocking their heads from side to side and rolling their eyes. They looked as if they were spaced out of their minds, thought Alice. All the girls were dancing. All the boys were standing round the edge of the room drinking Coke.

Cheryl came reluctantly at her mother's bidding, tossing her long mane of golden-brown hair back from her eyes.

'Oh, hi, Alice!' Her eyes fastened on the silver and blue parcel in Alice's hand.

Alice pushed it over. 'Happy birthday, Cheryl.'

'Gee, thanks, Alice. Nice you could come.' Cheryl was tearing off the glittery paper, mangling the rosette. What a waste of money, thought Alice. From the wreckage Cheryl lifted out the giant bottle of bubble bath. She laughed. 'Look, Mum! I'll have enough bubbles to keep me going till next year! Enough to drown me.'

'It was very nice of Alice to bring bubble bath,' said Ginny, who looked as if she might like to slap her daughter. A good idea, considered Alice.

Alice thought Cheryl had been referring to the size of her bottle but later, on going out into the hall, she saw amongst the display of Cheryl's presents five other bubble baths.

When the record ended Cheryl announced they were going to play Postman's Knock. The girls began to shriek and the boys to turn pink in the face. Alice wondered if she might go to the loo. Last time she'd been inveigled into going to a party, she'd spent half the time in the bathroom. She'd amused herself examining the contents of the hosts' medicine cabinet. It was amazing all the different things people had. Marge's was full of herbal remedies and vitamins.

'Oh, no, you don't, Alice Crabtree!' Cheryl snatched her by the arm and dragged her back. '*Everybody*'s got to play. Everybody's got to have a number. The boys can be the postmen first.'

The boys shuffled out into the lobby, horsing around as they went, pushing one another, and the girls, left in the room, sizzled with excitement. Alice was surprised not to see smoke issuing from the tops of their heads. Cheryl was going round breathing hotly into everyone's ear. Giving each of them a number. Alice received six. At least she presumed it was meant to be six. It had sounded more like 'sick'. A middling sort of number, six, she assessed, less likely to be called than some others. One, seven and ten would be the ones that would be called most. They'd come to mind more readily. She'd have been prepared to bet that Cheryl would have given herself one or seven.

Alice retreated to a corner by the window and looked out into the street. A couple of small girls were playing jumps over a rope. She wouldn't mind jumping a rope.

'Knock-knock!' Here came the first postman.

'Who's there?' demanded the girls, all but the one in the corner looking out.

'The postman.'

'Come in, Mr Postman!' they chorused in sing-song voices.

In came Teddy Black.

'Wow-wow,' went the girls, pretending to swoon. He was wearing a leather jacket even though it was a hot day, and he'd put grease on his hair. What a right looking twit! thought Alice. He was supposed to be the heart-throb of Cheryl's class, so Alice had over-heard in the playground. Cheryl was in a class below Alice, even though she was a few months older. Another piece of information Alice had gleaned was that Cheryl fancied Teddy.

Teddy was looking at Cheryl now and she was laughing and flicking her hair around her shoulders. Alice wondered if she practised it in front of the mirror.

'C'mon, Teddy!' shouted the girls. 'What number do you want?'

He was still deliberating.

'Don't tell him, Cheryl, don't tell him!' urged the others. 'Let him guess!'

'Ssss . . .' hissed Cheryl's friend Geraldine. 'Sss . . . eee . . .'

'Six!' cried Teddy.

What a fathead, thought Alice.

'Six,' repeated Cheryl, no longer laughing.

'Who's got six?' Everyone turned to everyone else.

'Not me,' they said. 'Not me.'

Alice was saying nothing. She was wondering if it

would be feasible to jump out of the window. There were some rose beds right outside but it should be easy enough to clear those. Anyway, a few thorns in the flesh would be preferable to having to kiss Teddy Black.

'Alice has got six,' said Cheryl in a voice that sounded accusing, as if it was Alice's fault.

'*Alice* has got six!' Shrieks of hyena-like laughter erupted around the room. 'Imagine – Alice! Teddy's picked the *professor*! Go on, Professor! Teach him a few things!'

'Don't want to,' she muttered.

'Spoil-sport, spoil-sport! Party-pooper, party-pooper!'

'Come *on*, Alice,' said Cheryl, taking hold of her arm. Her fingers dug in, her grip was like a vice. 'He picked your number. You've got to go through with it. Give me a hand, Geraldine.'

Geraldine, giggling, took Alice's other arm. Alice let her body go heavy, but she was smaller than either of them and light-weight, so it was fairly easy for them to drag her out into the hall where Teddy was lounging against the wall. The rest of the boys had been shut in the dining room but a slit of light showed at the edge of the door and several eyes were glued to it.

Cheryl gave Alice a shove in the back to propel her in Teddy's direction, then slipping her arm through Geraldine's she went back to the party room. As they shut the door behind them Cheryl said to Geraldine in a clear voice, 'I didn't want to ask her to the party, anyway. Mother made me. I can't *stand* spoil-sports.'

Alice looked at Teddy. She came up to about the middle of his chest. 'I'd rather not, if you don't mind.'

'I wouldn't kiss you if you paid me,' said Teddy, and barged his way into the dining room, sending bodies reeling at the back of the door.

Alice ran all the way home. Her mother was in the kitchen making a plum and apple pie.

'I hate you for making me go to that party!' Alice cried, and burst into tears.

Later, in her journal, she wrote, 'I suppose Cheryl was disappointed that Teddy hadn't chosen her number. And that's why she was so angry with me. I hate her now! She's left nasty red marks on my arm and I think they're going to bruise. Marge didn't get to put magical Arnica on it quickly enough. And Cheryl tore one of the sleeves of my dress. Though that doesn't matter, except that Mum could have given it to Oxfam.

'It was all so *silly*. One thing, Mum won't try to make me go to another party ever again. She was really upset and said she was going to complain to Ginny, but I made her swear cross her heart that she wouldn't as it would just end with them all laughing at me in the playground. And I won't have Lizzie there to stand up for me any more. Peter also said to Mum better not say anything to Ginny, it might spoil their friendship and they've been friends a long time, after all. So she sighed and said she guessed he was right, you had to take care of your friendships, they don't just grow on trees, like pieces of fruit to be plucked off when you feel like it.'

Alice stared gloomily at the page for a moment, then wrote, 'I guess I'll hold the record for the shortest time spent at a party,' and that cheered her up a bit.

TWELVE

'*I*'m fed up being an unpaid au pair girl,' Lizzie wrote in her diary. 'It's not fair!'

She lifted her pen as a tide of anger washed over her. She felt almost blinded by it. And then gradually it went off the boil, and was reduced to a simmer. But that simmer of resentment remained.

'She made me miss my date,' Lizzie scribbled at ferocious speed so that no one but her (or Alice) would be able to make out the writing. 'Why she ever had a child I can't imagine. Mrs A. says she told her she didn't want one, it was to please him. It was *her* fault, not his, that I missed my date. If it had been him he'd have said he'd come home straight away. He'd have said, "Of course you've got to go and meet Richard. You promised to meet him. You can't stand him up. I don't go for people standing one another up." He wouldn't have said, "Business, business, business! Nothing matters but money, money, money!" And now I probably won't have the chance to go out with Richard again. He won't want to go out with a girl who's stood him up.'

After Candice's call, Lizzie had burst into tears, alarming Cressy.

'What's wrong, Lizzie? What is it? Please don't cry.'

Lizzie had wanted to take it out on Cressy, which she knew wouldn't be fair. She'd wanted to shout at her, 'Your mother's a selfish bitch,' but she'd restrained herself and told Cressy to forget it, and she'd dried her tears and blown her nose and read the child a story.

Lizzie continued with her diary. 'I think I'm going to try and talk to Mark about it. He's so easy to talk to. Well, I should know that – I've talked to him in my head often enough! I'm going to tell him that I feel just like an au pair. I'm with Cressy from morning to night, I haven't got any life of my own. I can't go to the loo without her asking me where I'm going. I can hear Alice saying into my ear, "Go on, Lizzie, sock it to him!" I wouldn't mind Alice being here right now, I have to admit. For an hour or two, anyway. We might even be able to have a good laugh about it. As it is, I don't feel much like laughing! I'll try to put it to my father as nicely as I can —'

A tap on the door made her jump and cover the page with her hand.

'Are you awake, Lizzie?' asked Mark, putting his head round.

She hadn't heard them come in. She glanced at the digital clock beside her bed. It showed 11:10.

'I'm terribly sorry we're so late, really we hadn't intended to be. But they were very important clients and they asked us to have dinner with them afterwards. It was difficult to refuse.'

Lizzie nodded. Her throat was playing up again. She couldn't get any words out at all.

'Everything been all right here? No problems with Cressy?'

Lizzie shook her head.

'Are you free tomorrow night?'

Well, of course she was free! She didn't have a whole pack of friends here who'd come calling and asking her out. But she was on her guard straight away. Of course they would want to come home late again tomorrow, there would be more important clients to see, cocktail parties to go to in swish bars, dinners to eat in expensive restaurants.

'No, I'm sorry,' she said, finding her voice in a rush, 'I'm not. Some people I met at the sports club have asked me to go out with them.'

'That's a shame. Oh well, can't be helped. I was going to ask you to come out and have dinner with me, just the two of us, to give us the chance to talk a bit more. I feel I haven't had much time with you in the last week or so, we've been so snowed under with work. Cressy's going with Candice to visit her grandmother tomorrow. It's Granny's birthday, so I thought I'd just excuse myself and spend it with you. Never mind. Another time! Sleep well, Lizzie.' He bent down and kissed her cheek, and then he was gone.

Lizzie burst into tears for the second time that evening. Nothing seemed to be going her way, everything was stacked against her.

She had a restless, tormented night's sleep and got up early. She washed her face, pulled on her dressing-gown and went downstairs, hoping to catch her father on his own. He was sitting at the kitchen table with Candice. They were drinking coffee.

'Morning, Lizzie,' said Mark.

'Had a good sleep?' asked Candice, who had a sheet of paper in front of her and a pen in her hand. 'Sorry about last night, by the way, Lizzie. You did understand, didn't you? Now, Mark, the costings for the warehouse conversion . . .'

'Help yourself to coffee, Lizzie,' said Mark.

Lizzie sat opposite them, nursing her cup, wondering if she would be able to break into the conversation at any point. It seemed unlikely.

Suddenly the phone pealed out. It was like a gift from the gods for Candice sprang up at once to answer it.

'Hello. Oh, it's you, Mother.'

'Mark,' said Lizzie quickly, 'you know about tonight? Well, I was thinking I could cancel my date.'

'Oh, I wouldn't want you to do that. I mean, you missed out on last night's.'

Behind them, Candice went on murmuring.

'I know,' said Lizzie. 'But I'd rather go out with you, honestly I would.'

'Are you sure? Okay then, let's do it! What kind of food do you like?'

'Anything. Well, within reason,' she laughed. 'Not tripe or sweetbreads or stuff like that.'

'What about Thai? There's a very nice Thai restaurant just opened near our office. The food's delicious.'

'Fantastic!'

'Right, you're on!'

The phone pinged. 'That was Mother,' said Candice

unnecessarily. 'She's looking forward to seeing us all this evening.'

'But Lizzie and I have just made a date.'

'You told me Lizzie wasn't free to go out.'

'She's changed her mind! Mine was an offer she couldn't refuse.'

'But I've just told Mother that you're coming, Mark. She'll be very disappointed if you don't. I don't believe you came for her birthday last year, either.'

There was silence while Candice and Mark confronted one another. Lizzie held her breath.

'Lizzie will be disappointed if I pull out now,' said Mark quietly.

'I'm sure Lizzie wouldn't mind making it another time, would you, Lizzie?' said Candice. 'You can go out with your friends, as arranged.'

'No, Lizzie and I are going out tonight, and that's that,' said Mark, and he rose from the table. Lizzie sensed that it was not often he stood up to Candice.

He and Candice left for work without speaking.

Lizzie had a new daydream. Candice and Mark decide to separate, there's nothing else for it. He says to her, 'We haven't been getting on for a long time. I'm fed up with all this arguing.' She says to him, 'You're right,' and sighs. 'It's over between us, Mark. We can't go on pretending any longer. And it's not fair on Cressy to bring her up in such a bad atmosphere. I'll take Cressy.' 'And I'll take Lizzie,' he says.

'Have you had your breakfast?' demanded Cressy, coming bouncing into the kitchen. 'You might have woken me up.'

At intervals throughout the day Lizzie went on

with her daydream. She saw her father and herself living in a luxurious penthouse apartment, with a roof garden; in a cottage in the country with rambler roses climbing the walls; in a house with a veranda overlooking the sea. She saw them spending week-ends in London and in Paris . . .'

Every time the phone rang that day she almost jumped out of her skin in case it would be Candice to give her the usual story about being unavoidably delayed that evening etc. Or in case it would be Richard, who had somehow or other managed to find her phone number and was ringing up to ask if she was all right since she hadn't turned up for their date. And to ask for another one. But there were no calls from either Candice or Richard. And when Lizzie and Cressy went for their daily swim there was no sign of him at the club, or of Pam and Simon, either. They were probably off for the day, with some other girl making up the fourth.

Candice and Mark arrived home at six o'clock precisely. They were talking to one another again, but to Lizzie's ear Candice sounded cool.

'Go and get dressed now, Cressy,' said her mother. 'Wear your pretty pink dress, the one with the little white flowers. Granny likes you in that dress.'

Lizzie left Candice to oversee the dressing of Cressy and retired to her room to consider her own wardrobe. She didn't have all that much to choose from, and a lot of the better, more grown-up things had come from Candice. Tonight she was not going to wear anything of Candice's! She was going to be herself. She decided on a deep blue blouse and her white skirt.

Candice and Cressy left first, taking the smaller of the two cars. Shortly afterwards, Mark and Lizzie set off in the Mercedes. Wait till I write and tell Alice, thought Lizzie, she won't half be envious! It was like riding in an armchair.

The decor of the restaurant was interesting and attractive, as Lizzie had expected. She couldn't imagine her father going anywhere scruffy or ugly. Plants grew in pots, and trailed all round the room, their leaves glossily green. They gave the place a feeling of being out of doors. Lizzie and Mark were seated by a window looking into a courtyard, where geraniums bloomed in vivid scarlet and pure white. A waitress in Thai costume served them.

Mark guided Lizzie through the menu, making suggestions. He ordered wine. He was most attentive, asking her as each course came if it suited her, did she like that coconut taste, the spices weren't too hot for her, were they?

She liked everything. She couldn't remember ever having such a wonderful evening. Her father told her about himself when he was a boy, how he'd drawn all the time, on any old piece of paper, the backs of envelopes, the covers of jotters. His father had wanted him to go into his engineering business and he had hated the idea.

'Do you like to draw, Lizzie?'

'Yes, I do. I don't seem to have done much recently. It's funny, I've almost forgotten about it. Other things . . .'

'Have got in the way? I know. Life takes over and doesn't leave you enough time.'

He understands everything, she thought. He understands *me*.

'It's important to take time to live as well,' he said. 'One goes through different stages.'

She nodded.

'You'll probably come back to it.'

'I'd like to.'

'It wouldn't be terribly surprising if you were good at art, with both your mother and I being inclined that way. She was very talented at school, you know? Oh yes. She should have gone to art college herself.' He was sounding nostalgic, had a far-off look in his eyes. 'I feel guilty that she didn't.

'I was really very fond of your mother, I want you to know that. It wasn't casual, our relationship. We met at the wrong time. That happens. We met too young . . .'

The minutes, hours, ticked by. Mark had gone back in time, to before he'd met Candice. To the time of his youth, when he was Lizzie's age and a little older, when he was carefree and in love with Lizzie's mother. A golden time, he called it, laughing a little at himself, yet believing it, she could tell that. She felt very close to him. The restaurant emptied, until theirs was the only table left occupied. In the background, the waitress yawned.

Mark blinked suddenly and looked round the room. 'I guess we'd better go. We must be keeping them out of their beds.' He smiled at Lizzie. 'For a moment there I thought you were your mother!'

It was only when he was calling for the bill that Lizzie remembered that she had planned to speak to him. About being treated like an au pair girl. She had rehearsed her speech in her head so that she would sound reasonable. She wasn't going to fly off the handle! Certainly not. That was the old Lizzie that she'd left back in her other home.

She looked at her father across the table. He was leaning back in his chair and smiling at her and saying how much he'd enjoyed her company.

'It's been great, Lizzie.'

'For me, too.'

She couldn't possible say anything now. If she did, she would spoil the evening. One of the best evenings of her life.

THIRTEEN

'*D*ear Alice,
    You are invited to a party.'
    Alice groaned. Not again!
    Marge looked up from the muesli pottery bowl that
Ginny had designed and fired in a burst of going to
evening classes. It didn't sit quite level on the table and
bulged at one side. 'What's up with you? Not feeling
well?'
    'I'm fine!'
    'Who's your letter from?'
    'Just a girl.'
    'In your class?'
    'Yes.'
    'Oh.'
    That 'Oh' was not really meant as a comment, or to
conclude their exchange, but as a question. A string of
questions. Who is she? Why is she writing a letter to
you? What does she want? Alice had no intention of
revealing that she'd been invited to another party, in
case her mother would start badgering her. *Well,*

perhaps you could give it a try? After all, you never know, you might like this one. Not all parties are the same. Trouble was Marge liked parties. She only needed a couple of friends to drop in and she'd say, 'Let's have a party!' And the next thing you knew Peter would be dispatched to the wine shop round the corner and a pizza delivery would be on its way. Actually, Alice didn't mind those sorts of parties. She wasn't expected to *do* anything much, except pass the pizza and talk to people.

She folded up the sheet of pale pink note paper and stuck it in the pocket of her shirt.

'I'd better be getting along to the shop. Dad'll be wondering where I am.'

'See you at lunch-time. Get a couple of pints of milk on your way back.'

'Okay.'

'And don't be late!'

Once Alice was round the corner and out of sight (of her mother), she took the letter from her pocket. She was invited to Sharon's birthday party a week on Saturday.

'We're going for a day's outing to the sea in our mini van. Do hope you can come. R.S.V.P.'

Sharon had been one of the girls at Cheryl's party. Alice couldn't understand it. Why would Sharon want to ask *her* to her birthday party?

Mrs Kelly was behind the counter reading *Hello* magazine. She loved reading about the rich and famous, and always concluded her reading by saying, 'It's all right for them!'

She put her thumb in the page to keep her place.

'Your dad's gone out on a message. There's some new stock in. He said maybe you could unpack it?'

While Alice was putting up tins of Coke and Sprite on the shelves she thought about Sharon's invitation and was half tempted to accept. Only half, though. She liked the sea, loved swimming and puddling about in rock pools and looking for pearly, translucent shells. That bit would be all right. But not the mini van packed with shrilling, giggly girls like Cheryl and stupid oafs like Teddy.

Zac arrived shortly afterwards with his emptied paper sack. He nodded over at Alice. 'Something to tell you,' he mouthed.

She followed him through to the back.

'Is it a stamp fair?'

'Yep! A week on Saturday.'

'Week on Saturday? That settles it, then.'

'Settles what?'

'Oh, just that I had an invitation to a party. But I'd *far* rather go to a stamp fair.'

'Wait till you hear where it is!' He was grinning, as if he was in possession of a tantalising secret.

'It's not here, is it? In town? Come on, Zachary Hornbeam, stop grinning like an oaf!'

He told her then where the fair was to be held.

'But that's where Markie and Candy Floss and Mustard Face live! That's where *Lizzie* is.'

'I know!'

'We could go and see Lizzie,' said Alice slowly.

'That's what I was thinking.'

'We could surprise her!'

When Peter came in, Alice told him about the fair. 'I want to go, Dad. *Please*! Can I?'

'It's a long way,' he said dubiously. 'Couple of hours on the train there and back.'

'We might be able to stay the night at Lizzie's.' It was not Lizzie's place, of course, and they were both well aware of that.

'We wouldn't want to impose on them.' Peter didn't seem to like that idea at all.

'Well, we could easily make it in a day. No problem. And I've got the money saved for the fare. *Please*, Dad! Do say yes, I'll die if you don't!'

'We'll need to see what your mother says.'

Alice had hoped her father would have said that he'd back her. It would have strengthened her arm with her mother. Marge could be unreasonable at times. Irrational.

Alice could think of nothing else but the stamp fair all morning. She left sharp at lunch-time, bought the milk, didn't stop chatting with Khalil, and she made no detours.

As she was coming out of the shop carrying her milk, she ran into Sharon. The piece of pink paper was still sticking out of her shirt pocket.

Sharon greeted her in a very friendly way. 'Did you get my invitation, Alice?'

'Oh yes, I did, thanks. But I can't come, I'm afraid.'

'Oh, you can't? I'm sorry.'

'No, I'm going to a big stamp fair that day, you see. It's to be a really big fair, with dealers from all over.'

'You're not a dealer?'

'Oh, no. Just a collector.'

'Oh, well. Maybe another time.'

Sharon was going the same way. She fell into step beside Alice. She was the second smallest in their class and not much taller than Alice. When it came to having photographs taken they were put together in the middle of the front row.

'I haven't asked Cheryl to my party.'

'No?'

'No. I thought she was horrible to you at her party.'

So that's why she's asked me, thought Alice. She felt sorry for me!

'I'm only having half a dozen girls. I didn't want a rowdy party like Cheryl's. So my dad said what about a day at the sea?'

'Should be nice.'

'I expect you'll have a good time at your stamp fair, though.'

'I expect so.'

They said cheerio and Alice turned in at her gate.

Marge was in the kitchen cooking pasta.

'Can I ask you something, Mum?' asked Alice straight away, unable to wait a moment longer.

'Just a second till I pour the spaghetti!'

A cloud of steam enveloped Marge's head as she tipped the pasta into a colander. Alice moved round to her other side and positioned herself at the draining board.

'You remember I said Zac was going to take me to a stamp fair?'

'I believe you said something –' Marge broke off to shout at Jamie who was about to put a fork in his mouth. 'Take that fork off him, Alice!'

Alice removed the fork and went back on the attack. If you wanted to get anything through to Marge you had to persist. You were liable to be interrupted every two seconds. In a rush she rattled off all the details.

Marge set down the colander. 'But that's a long way for you to go on your own. It must be a hundred miles.'

'I'm not going on my own. I'm going with Zac.'

'He's not old enough to look after you.'

'He is! He's fifteen.'

'He's a bit scatty, is Zac, always has his head in the clouds. Not overly mature for his age. It'd be too big a responsibility for him.'

'No, it wouldn't, Mum.' Alice felt like grinding her teeth. Or stamping her foot. But neither would get her anywhere. 'You'd have let me go with Lizzie.'

'He's not Lizzie.'

'But he's the same age.'

'Let me get the lunch served or the spaghetti'll be cold. Damn, it's stuck together! I forgot to put a little oil in the water. It was you talking to me that took my mind off it.'

So it's my fault now that the spaghetti has glued itself together! thought Alice.

She brought Johnny to the table, lifted Jamie into his high chair and tied his bib. Anything to curry favour. Her mother served the pasta.

'Get the parmesan out of the fridge,' said Marge.

Alice got it and placed it where Johnny wouldn't be able to reach it.

'Please, Mum, let me go,' she pleaded. 'I'll be ever

so careful, I'll stick close by Zac and I won't speak to any strange men or women and I won't stand too close to the edge of the platform.'

'You can go to a stamp fair some other time. When there's one nearer at hand.'

'I want to go to this one! I could go and see Lizzie at the same time.'

'I don't know about that.' Marge was frowning now and she had a guarded look in her eye. 'I mean, you'd need to be invited. You can't just barge in. It's obviously not that kind of household. And then there's Zac as well. No, I don't think it's a good idea.'

'You don't want me to meet *them*, do you? That's the real reason! But it's not as if I'm going to *stay* there and not come back. Like Lizzie.'

Marge stared at her. She looked appalled. She hates the idea of Lizzie not coming back, thought Alice. She's not reconciled to it at all, even though she says she is and goes on about letting Lizzie choose how to lead her own life.

'He's not *my* father,' said Alice, feeling desperate. 'He won't want me. There's no danger of me going over to the enemy camp.'

'It's nothing to do with enemies! Or camps.'

'Well, then, if it's not, what's the problem?'

'Alice, I don't want to hear one more word about it. Not *one*. The answer is no!'

FOURTEEN

'You're always drawing these days,' said Cressy. 'Who's that you're doing now?'

'My sister. Alice.'

'I'm your sister too, though, aren't I?' Cressy had changed her mind about that.

'You are indeed my sister.' Lizzie began to draw Alice's spectacles, perched half-way down her nose.

'What's she like? Alice?'

'Sort of quirky.'

'What does that mean?'

'Some people think she's odd.'

'Do you think she is?'

'No!'

'Do you like me better than her?'

'It's not a case of better or worse. But I do like *you*, Cressy.' And Lizzie realised that she did, in spite of all the numerous ways the child could annoy her. She felt sorry for Cressy. Her mother paid her hardly any attention and Cressy so badly wanted to please her. She would stand on her head for an hour if she thought it would make her mother smile.

Lizzie finished shading Alice's hair and held the drawing at arm's length.

'Does it look like her?' asked Cressy.

'Yes, I think it does!'

'Can I have it?'

''Fraid not. I'm going to pin it up.' Lizzie took a thumb tack and stapled the piece of paper to her notice board, alongside a drawing of Marge and Peter. It was funny, she'd been doodling around one day, not thinking about anything in particular and, suddenly, there they both were taking shape at the end of her pencil: Marge frowning, looking thoughtful, Peter leaning back with his hands behind his head.

Mark had come in and seen it and said, 'You've caught her likeness. Do you get on well together, the two of you?'

'When we're apart,' Lizzie had said, and felt guilty afterwards. They'd written a couple of letters to each other, she and her mother, casual newsy letters, nothing emotional. They'd kept well clear of danger areas. Like how they were feeling about each other. And Lizzie hadn't phoned home after that first day; she felt she couldn't cope with the sound of their voices.

'Will you draw me sometime and put me on the wall?' asked Cressy.

Lizzie promised that she would.

She put away her sketch book and pencils and took out her bathing costume. Cressy was already waiting to go swimming, had her suit and towel rolled up like a sausage underneath her arm.

The pool was quiet today. One man was crawling

106

up and down the far lane, splintering the smooth turquoise expanse of water. And sitting on the edge of the pool with his feet dangling was Richard. He was staring at his feet. The sight of him gave Lizzie a shock. He was alone.

'You've gone all pink, Lizzie,' said Cressy.

Lizzie looked across at Richard under lowered eyelids. He probably wouldn't want to know her. If it hadn't been for Cressy she would have spun around and slipped back into the dressing rooms. As it was, she would have to stand her ground. She felt her legs tremble a little. Silly fool! Then he glanced up and saw her and raised his hand in salutation. And so there seemed nothing else to do but to take Cressy by the hand and walk around the pool to speak to him.

'I was wondering if I was going to see you again,' he said.

'Richard, I'm sorry about that night,' Lizzie said quickly, and went on to explain.

He said he understood, he hadn't thought she'd just stood him up, he'd known there must have been some reasonable explanation. He would never expect to be stood up, she thought. Whereas she, in a similar situation, would have thought just that.

'But I didn't know how to get in touch with you.'

'Nor I you.'

Cressy was tugging at Lizzie's hand. 'Come on, Lizzie! I want to go down the shute. You promised, didn't you?'

'Guess I did.'

'You'd better go with her.' Richard grinned. 'What about a date tonight or tomorrow night?'

'Tomorrow,' said Lizzie. She knew Mark and Candice would be at home. They were having a couple of friends in for a meal. Candice had said she would invite Lizzie but she thought she'd be 'bored out of her mind'.

That evening, Mark and Candice were home early and they all ate together. Candice made spaghetti carbonara, Cressy's favourite. Candice could cook quickly and well, when she wanted to, and had time. They had a pleasant meal. Lizzie brought up the subject of her date for the next day.

'Lizzie's in love,' said Cressy.

Lizzie felt her face grow hot. 'I am not! I hardly know him.' Her father was smiling.

'There's no problem about tomorrow,' said Candice.

'I'm going out at seven,' said Lizzie firmly. She had decided she must be firm, that Candice would respect her more if she was.

'We'll have to be back in good time for our dinner party, anyway.'

'Not fair!' grumbled Cressy. 'What will I do?'

'You, my sweet, will go to bed. You're only seven, remember!'

Really, Candice was all right, thought Lizzie, when she went up to her room after Cressy had gone to bed. Candice could be generous. She had just given her a pair of blue dangly earrings to match her blouse. She'd pulled them from the drawer and said, 'Here, have these! You'd look good in them. Wear them for your date.' Lizzie had come to the conclusion that she liked Candice most of the time, which was as much as you could expect with anybody. Except her father. She liked him all of the time; he'd never said a word to annoy her, not once. And Richard, she liked him too. She caught Alice's eye looking at her over the top of her spectacles and grinned at her. 'Okay, Alice, for all the time that I've known him. Which I admit is not much.'

Lizzie got on well with Richard right from their first date. He admired her hair, said he liked her earrings. She found him easy to be with altogether. He didn't seem to have score points or brag in order to try to impress her, the way she'd found a lot of boys did. He asked her what she'd like to do.

'Anything,' she said. 'It's your home ground. You choose.'

He was hungry. They ate at a burger joint and then afterwards went for a walk along the river. It was a balmy evening, the kind that made you want to drift along and not hurry. They talked non-stop, filling in the details of their lives for one another, and they laughed a lot. They had fun, as Lizzie wrote to her friend Carol the next day. 'And he's gorgeous!' she added, drawing a little picture of him at the foot of the letter.

She saw Richard every day that week, at some point or other, sometimes in the morning or afternoon when she was with Cressy, but every evening on her own. When Candice or Mark were out he came along and helped baby-sit. Candice and Mark said that was fine by them. They liked him, thought him nice-man-nered and considerate, and mature for his age. (He was a year older than Lizzie.) He joined them for dinner one evening on the terrace and he helped Mark at the barbecue. He was at ease chatting to both Mark and Candice, was not at all gauche. Lizzie thought of Zac. He'd have been falling over everything, dropping steaks on the grass, burning his hand on the coals.

On Saturday morning, Lizzie wrote up her diary for the week. She'd been too busy to do it daily.

'Everything's going really well now. I feel I'm settling in and having a life of my own and they're not treating me simply as an au pair. Well, not too much. At times I still feel she's making use of me and when she wants something she turns on the charm. And then I think maybe I'm not being fair to her. I just don't know! I suppose it wasn't easy for her to have me here even though she said she didn't mind. But I feel more on a level with them. And they've been coming home quite early most days so that Richard and I are free to go out.'

Richard and I. Lizzie smiled. It had a nice ring to it.

'Lizzie!' She heard Mark calling from below,

She went out on to the landing.

'Could we have a word, Lizzie? Can you come down? Something's cropped up.'

They were in the kitchen. Candice was pacing up and down with one hand up to her face and the other supporting her elbow. She seemed tense. A frown corrugated her brow.

'Lizzie, we've just had a call from Milan,' said Mark.

She had heard the phone go a couple of times.

'We've got an emergency on our hands,' said Candice. 'We'll have to go over and sort things out. Too much is at stake.'

'It's a big job,' said Mark.

'One of the biggest we've ever had.'

'When do you have to go?' asked Lizzie.

'Tomorrow morning.'

'*Tomorrow?*'

'We've phoned the travel agent and he can get us on a flight. Last two tickets.'

'We've no option but to take them,' said Mark.

'How long will you be gone for?'

'Four days, five. A week, possibly.'

'So you want me to look after Cressy on my *own* for a week?'

'Oh no, we wouldn't leave you on your own, Lizzie, ' said Mark. 'You're capable, we know that, but we wouldn't dream of asking you to carry that responsibility. So we've asked my mother to come over and keep you company.'

'It'll give you a chance to get to know your grandmother,' said Candice.

Lizzie thought she could detect a little smile at the corner of Candice's mouth.

FIFTEEN

'*M*um,' said Alice, 'you remember I got a letter from a girl a few days ago?' She extracted the sheet of pink paper from her pocket. By now it was looking somewhat rumpled. She straightened it out and laid it on the table so that her mother could read it if she wished.

'Oh, yes. From a girl in your class?'

'Sharon Wood. She lives in Cranbourne Gardens.'

'I wonder if that's Linda Wood's daughter. She used to be in my yoga class.'

Oh no! Trust her mother to know Sharon's mother! That could be tricky.

'No, maybe she lived in Ashley Drive. And I think she had two boys.'

Thank goodness for that! Alice breathed more easily again, and said, 'Sharon's asked me to her birthday party.'

'You're not thinking of going?' Marge looked up from the ironing board where she was ironing her red silk blouse. She was having a night out with Ginny;

they were going to a French restaurant downtown. It had to be something special before Marge got the ironing board out. 'You're thinking of going to a party?'

'Mind you don't burn your blouse! I was thinking I *might* go. It's not the usual kind of party, there are to be just six girls, and they're going to the seaside. In Mr Wood's mini van. Mrs Wood's going too. She's very nice. And responsible. I think she might even be a social worker. They're going to have a picnic on the beach.'

'Sounds all right to me. When is it?'

'Saturday. They're leaving early in the morning, coming back in the evening. It's to be a whole day out.'

'You always enjoy the sea and we don't get much chance to go with the shop being open six and a half days a week. What a tie that is! We haven't had a holiday for three years. Next year! Still, we've got to eat. Why don't you accept, love? It'd make a change for you.'

'Perhaps I will,' said Alice diffidently. 'At least it won't be silly games.'

'By the way, did I tell you that Cheryl had told Ginny you'd left her party because you weren't feeling well? I didn't disillusion her. Tell you what, if you go to Sharon's party, I'll buy you a new top.'

'Bribery and corruption,' would have been Alice's normal response. As it was, she just said, 'Thanks, Mum,' and sidled out of the kitchen.

She went out into the garden and stood on an old seed box so that she could see over the wall into Zac's garden. He was in the yard working on his bicycle. He had it up-ended and one wheel off. She hoped he knew how to put it back together again.

'Hi, Zac! Hey, are you still going to the stamp fair on Saturday?'

'Thought I would.' He pushed a lock of tow-coloured hair out of his eyes with a greasy fist, and left a black streak on his forehead. 'It should be a good one. Pity you can't come.'

'It is, isn't it?' She sighed. 'What train are you catching?'

'Nine o'clock. That means I'd get there at eleven. Wouldn't want to leave it much later.'

'No, you wouldn't, would you? You might miss too much. What train'll you get back?'

'Depends. They run every hour. Last one's eight. I'd get one before that, though, maybe the six.'

'Seven hours then,' said Alice, 'from eleven until six.'

Next afternoon, Marge took Alice shopping downtown. She left the two boys at a friend's; they had a mutual child-swapping arrangement.

'We might as well enjoy ourselves,' said Marge. 'And we can go and have a cup of coffee afterwards, in peace!'

She bought Alice a top in a soft shade of yellow and a hair band to match. 'Now we'll need to buy a birthday present for Sharon.'

'It doesn't have to be anything much,' said Alice, feeling uncomfortable. 'A pair of socks would do.'

'I don't want to be thought a cheapskate! What

about bubble bath? Ginny says all the girls like smelly things like that.'

'Not bubble bath.'

They settled on an inexpensive blue tee-shirt.

In the café, over a cappuccino and a banana milk shake, Marge said, 'I still can't get used to the idea of not having Lizzie around. Even though she was such a pain in the neck for the last year. I bet she's all sweetness and light in his place. It's always the way. People tell you how *nice* your kids are in their house. What did she say in her letter this morning?'

'It was all Richard. Richard says this, Richard says that. She seems to think he's an oracle.'

'Oh, well,' said Marge, looking wistful. 'I expect she'll come back and visit us sometime.'

When she got home Alice washed the better of her two pairs of jeans, and on Friday evening gave them a good iron.

'You are taking the party seriously, aren't you?' said her mother. 'I thought you usually just finished them off in the dryer?'

Alice shrugged.

'You'd better take your anorak. The forecast's not all that brilliant for tomorrow, unfortunately. It's a shame, especially when we've having such a good run of weather. I suppose they'll go, anyway?'

'Oh, yes, I'm sure they will! There's lots to do inside.'

'I hope they wouldn't take you into those awful amusement arcades!'

'Oh no, they wouldn't do that. They're not like that at all.'

'Do you think I should go round and have a word with Mrs Wood?'

'No need,' said Alice hastily. 'You've got plenty to do.'

'Don't forget to wrap Sharon's present. Did you bring paper from the shop?'

Alice took out the orange and yellow striped wrapping paper and carefully wrapped up the blue tee-shirt. Her fingers were a little jittery and she got the sellotape tangled up in the paper.

'Not like you,' said her mother. 'Not nervous about going tomorrow, are you? I'm sure you don't have to be. It's not going to be like Cheryl's, remember!'

Alice went up to bed early. The anticipation was exhausting her. She put only a brief entry into her journal. 'Sometimes you don't have any option, you have to do something you don't quite approve of.'

She slept as soon as she lay down, and the next thing she knew, Peter was shaking her and saying, 'You wanted wakened early, didn't you? I'm just off to the shop, dear. Have a good time at your party!'

She had a shower and dressed and went downstairs. No one else was up. The boys had gone late to bed (a not uncommon occurrence), which meant that they would sleep late in the morning and that would give Marge the chance for a bit of a lie-in. Alice didn't feel like any breakfast but thought she'd better eat something, it was going to be a long day. She ate half a bowl of Rice Crispies. Muesli would be too much to swallow and toast might stick in her throat. Then, after making sure that her mother was not stirring, she quickly made two rounds of sandwiches, one of cheese and pickle and the other lettuce and tomato. She wrapped them up and put them in the bottom of her drawstring bag, underneath her purse and Sharon's birthday present.

She tiptoed upstairs, tapped on her mother's door.

'That you, Alice?' Marge sounded half asleep still.

Alice opened the door a crack. 'I'm off then, Mum.'

'Okay. What time did you say you'd be back?'

'Half past eight or nine. Don't worry if we're a bit late, though. The traffic could be heavy.'

'Have a good day! Don't swim too far out!'

'Don't worry. I won't.'

Alice shut the door quietly, fled back down the stairs and let herself out. She was on the early side but better that than arriving at the last minute. And she couldn't hang around in the house any longer. She glanced at Zac's house. No sign of life there. The front curtains upstairs and down were still drawn. Zac slept at the back.

She met no one she knew on the way up to the main road, and a bus came immediately. That was lucky! She leapt on board, had her fare ready in her hand. When they were passing the paper shop she put her head down between her knees and pretended to be tying the lace of her trainers.

She arrived at the station just after half past eight. There was a queue in the ticket office. She joined it and shuffled her way up to the windows with the rest. When it was her turn she produced her money and asked for a half-fare saver return. The ticket was pushed through the grill to her, no questions asked.

It was a quarter to nine. She was beginning to be a

little worried. The train was in, waiting at platform six. Passengers were boarding. She went outside and stood on the forecourt, scanning the steady stream of people coming down the slope. Ten to. What should she do? Get on the train by herself?

Then she saw Zac, running, weaving in and out of the crowd, his head bobbing to right and left. She waved at him.

'You're going to be late,' she cried. 'Have you got your ticket?'

'Yes,' he gasped. 'But what are you doing here, Allie? I thought you weren't allowed to go?'

'Never mind about that! Just come on, or we'll miss the train!'

SIXTEEN

'*T*his has not been an easy week,' Lizzie wrote in her diary on Saturday morning. 'I could even say it has been difficult! Thank goodness they'll be back tomorrow. Should be back tomorrow. Surely they *will* be back tomorrow.'

Mrs Wheeler – *Granny* Wheeler – had arrived on the previous Sunday morning only ten minutes before Mark and Candice set out for Milan. Granny Grumble, Lizzie had dubbed her straight away, though her bark had subsequently proved worse than her bite.

'It was so good of you to come, Mother, especially at such short notice,' said Mark, welcoming her, and Lizzie saw the woman's face soften. She would do anything for him, thought Lizzie.

'We really do appreciate it,' said Candice, pausing briefly as she flew around the house gathering up bits and pieces.

'I had a terrible drive up the motorway. Fog for the first hour. Then bad drivers all the way, no consideration. Sunday drivers. They shouldn't let half of them out on the roads . . .' Mrs Wheeler stopped as she registered Lizzie's presence. 'You must be —?'

'Mother, this is Lizzie,' said Mark.

Mrs Wheeler nodded at Lizzie. It was a long, slow nod.

'We simply must go, Mark,' said Candice. 'We can't afford to miss that flight. 'Bye, Mother, and thank you again. 'Bye, Lizzie, hope you have a good week. 'Bye, Cressy love, be good!' She bent to kiss the child.

Then they were off, with Cressy and Lizzie waving goodbye from the front doorstep, and Mrs Wheeler remaining in the kitchen. Mark tooted the horn as they turned out of the drive. Cressy slipped her hand into Lizzie's.

'I wish they'd asked Granny Blair to come,' she said. That was Candice's mother.

'Shush,' cautioned Lizzie, for she didn't doubt but that Granny Wheeler would have sharp ears. And now that she had seen *her* grandmother, she wished it could have been the other granny, too. She liked Granny Blair. She was a sweet little woman, but a bit wandery in the head, and she was inclined to burn things on the stove, which meant that she was ruled out as a child-minder. She also had a husband to consider, after a fashion. Grandpa Blair spent most of his time in the garden under a bee veil; he had six hives and two sheds full of stored honey.

'I could be doing with a cup of tea,' said Mrs Wheeler, who had wedged herself into the kitchen rocking chair. 'I've been driving for the last couple of hours. I was up at the crack.'

'I'll put the kettle on,' said Lizzie, feeling all thumbs and no fingers.

'So they call you Lizzie? I suppose your proper name's Elizabeth?'

'No. I was christened Lizzie.'

'You don't tell me! Sounds a bit like your mother, I must admit. I knew your mother as a girl.'

'I know.'

Lizzie poured a cup of tea with hands that were not quite steady and set it with the milk jug and sugar basin in front of Granny Wheeler.

'I like my milk in before the tea.'

'Oh, I'm sorry.' Lizzie made to remove the cup.

'It's all right, you can leave it this time. I could be doing with a bit of toast, though, if you wouldn't mind. I've had nothing to eat since breakfast.'

Lizzie made two slices of toast, which Granny Grumble ate, dripping with butter and honey. Afterwards, her chin glistened. She was a large woman, and more than filled the rocking chair.

'Grandpa Blair made the honey,' said Cressy.

'The bees made the honey, Cressida,' her grandmother corrected her.

'That's what I meant.'

'That's not what you said. Always say what you mean and mean what you say.' Mrs Wheeler glanced along the draining board. 'What are we having for our lunch, then?'

'Candice has left a chicken.'

'It's about time you were getting it on, isn't it? If we're to eat at a civilised time.'

What time was civilised? Lizzie wondered, as she

stood at the sink peeling potatoes. Her mother would gawk with disbelief if she could see her. Why had Mrs Allison chosen to take her holiday this week of all weeks!

Mrs Wheeler had taken Cressy upstairs with her to help her unpack. Cressy had trailed after her unwillingly.

When the phone rang, it was Richard, as Lizzie had expected.

'No, I don't think I can meet you during the day, Richard.' She had hoped that Granny Wheeler might take Cressy to the park, might want to do grandmotherly things with her. 'Wait till you see her! She's a real cow.'

The door opened at her back, making her jump. Heat rushed into her face. 'Come round at eight,' she said and hung up.

'Who was that on the phone?'

'My boyfriend, Richard.'

'So you've got a boyfriend, have you?' *Didn't take you long, did it?* Was that what the woman was implying. Or was she being too sensitive? Possibly. For it was an odd situation to be in, meeting your grandmother for the first time, especially when she'd probably talked her son out of marrying your mother.

Lizzie threw the potatoes into the pot.

'So how's your mother?' asked her grandmother.

'Very well.'

'She's got other family, Mark says?'

'Three.'

'You must be enjoying staying here?'

'Yes.'

'It was good of Mark to take you in.'

'Yes,' said Lizzie, not liking the suggestion that she'd been 'taken in'. As if she'd been standing out in the cold with no other home to go to, like an orphan, rapping on the window pane, pleading to be let in.

'Candice, too. Not every woman would have taken you, under the circumstances.'

'No.' Lizzie began to scrape the carrots. 'I suppose not.'

'I was a bit surprised at her, I must say.'

Lizzie scraped more furiously. Careful now, she told herself, say nothing that you'll regret later! She's just a silly woman who opens her mouth and lets garbage fall out.

When Lizzie, hot and red-faced from bending over the oven, set the chicken on the table for Mrs Wheeler to carve, they found that it was still bright pink in the leg joints.

'Look at that! There's blood flowing.' Mrs Wheeler held the knife down to let blood ooze against the blade. 'You should have cut the legs open half an hour before the end. It's dangerous to eat half-cooked chicken. We could all get salmonella. Woman along my road got it, was on a drip and a ventilator. Couldn't get her breath. Did your mother never teach you how to cook a bird?'

It was the first time Lizzie had cooked a chicken, but she did not say so. She put the bird back in the oven for another twenty minutes. She burned her hand as she slid the roasting tin on to the shelf.

'Now the vegetables will be ruined,' grumbled Granny Grumble. 'I can't abide soggy veg.'

When the lunch was finally ready Cressy said she didn't want any chicken. She didn't want to go on a drip.

'Kids these days are far too fussy about their food,' said Granny Wheeler, as she held a chicken leg down with her fork and attacked it with her knife. 'They eat far too much rubbish. You see them going along my road eating pizzas and bags of crisps and bars of chocolate by the dozen. Munching like hamsters. Chomp, chomp, chomp. No wonder the nation's teeth are in decay! And then I get the dirty bags and wrappers to pick up afterwards in my garden.'

Lizzie found she did not have too much appetite, either.

She cooked every meal they ate that week, except for one that Granny Wheeler made, after which Lizzie decided she'd rather do the cooking herself. Granny's concoction was some kind of lamb stew floating in grease and riddled with bits of gristle. At least the cook herself had the good grace to acknowledge that it was terrible.

'I don't cook much these days. You get out of the way, when you live alone. Now when Mark was at home . . .'

Mark had not been at home for a very long time.

'When he comes I always get in a nice piece of rib of beef. I ask the butcher to cut it special. "Your son must be coming, Mrs Wheeler!" he'll say to me. Not that he manages to come that often.' His mother's voice had dropped, had sounded even a little accusing. She pulled herself up. 'He's a very busy man, of course. They're real business people, the pair of them.'

For the first time Lizzie felt sorry for the woman and was uncomfortable that she did. She wanted to be on her father's side and yet she was thinking that he really should go and visit his mother more often. Cressida hadn't seen her grandmother for nearly six months, until this week. Yet when Mark had summoned his mother she'd come, straight away. Grumbling. But she'd come.

Granny Wheeler took to Richard, once she'd given him the third degree. What does your father do? What are *you* going to do when you leave school? Don't you have a holiday job? What are your intentions towards my granddaughter? No, she hadn't gone quite that far! Nor was Lizzie sure that she'd think of her as her granddaughter. Richard knew how to deal with Mrs Wheeler. He stayed cool, answered her questions as if she'd every right to ask them, and gave her his charming smile.

'He reminds me of Mark a bit, you know, when he was a boy,' she said afterwards to Lizzie.

She liked to reminisce about Mark's boyhood and Lizzie liked to listen. After Cressy had gone to bed they'd sit together and Granny would pour herself a glass of sherry.

'He was popular at school, him being so clever and artistic, and captain of the rugby team. Good at everything, he was. The girls were always after him!'

'I'm sure my mother was never *after* him,' said Lizzie, flushing. 'It's not her style.'

Granny looked discomfited for a moment. 'No, maybe not. Yes, Marge was different. More mature than the others.'

'He fell in love with her. He said so.'

'Perhaps he did. But he was too young to be serious with a girl. He had other plans for his life. Marge knew that, she should have —' She broke off.

'Should have what?'

'Known better.'

'You mean it was all her fault? *I* was her fault?' A mistake? thought Lizzie. A nuisance. Someone who shouldn't really be here.

'I always say it's up to the girl —'

'That's ridiculous!'

'You've got Marge's temper anyway, that's for sure!'

Lizzie stormed out of the room.

SEVENTEEN

'*T*his one's cheese and pickle,' said Alice, passing it over. 'Cheddar.'

Zac hadn't brought any sandwiches, he hadn't thought to. But he'd bought crisps and drinks from the buffet car. He wouldn't have had time to make sandwiches, anyway, even if he had thought. He'd slept in.

'I almost came and threw gravel at your window. You know you read about doing it in books? I'd like to have seen if it works.'

'I sleep like the dead. That's what my mum says.'

'Probably wouldn't, then.'

They munched on their sandwiches. They had two airline-type seats so had no one opposite them.

'I don't like the idea of you doing this. There'll be all hell let loose when they find out. They'll probably blame me,' said Zac gloomily.

'No, they won't.'

'They always blame me.'

'I'll come clean if I have to. But there's no need for

them to find out. Sharon will be away all day and they're not coming back till about nine. So there's no way they can check up there. What would they check for, anyway?'

'I suppose they trust you.'

Now Alice felt gloomy. 'I didn't like telling lies, I admit that. But sometimes, when the stakes are high enough, you have to tell a white one.'

'This one's soot black. You must have wanted to go to the fair pretty badly.'

'I want to see Lizzie even more.'

'So that's it, is it! We're going to see Lizzie?'

'We'll go to the fair first.'

'That's good of you.'

'Don't mention it.'

Alice settled back to enjoy the ride. She decided she might as well, there was no point in feeling guilty all the way. And it wasn't often she got the chance of a train journey. She liked journeys, got a kick out of seeing new places, even fleetingly, passing through. She didn't mind too much, either, when they broke down and a new engine had to be brought, though Zac fretted a little, thinking of all the time he was missing at the fair.

They made up five minutes and reached their destination twenty-three minutes late. It was raining as they came out of the station.

'Just as well you didn't go to the seaside,' said Zac.

Neither of their anoraks had hoods. They stood under the shelter of the roof overhang, watching the rain bounce off the pavement and start to puddle the gutters. It was good, vigorous summer rain, marking the end of a long dry spell. They heard the crack of thunder.

'Now where?' asked Alice. 'Do we walk or get a bus? Have you got the address?'

Zac flapped the pockets of his anorak, then scrabbled inside them.

'What's up?' asked Alice.

'Can't seem to find the piece of paper. I'm sure I put it in.'

'You're not sure at all, are you? Can't you *remember* the address, for goodness sake?'

'It must be somewhere central. The place.' Now he was investigating the pockets of his jeans.

'Honestly, Zachary Hornbeam, you are the end!'

'Not everyone can have a phenomenal memory like you, Miss Mastermind!'

'We'll just have to ask.'

They went back into the station to Information, but they were only informing on train arrivals and departures and delays. They said try the Central Halls in Hill Street, sometimes antique fairs were held there. 'Turn left when you come out of the station, then right at the third set of traffic lights and go up the hill. That's Hill Street.'

It was still raining. By the time they arrived at the Central Halls their heads were as sleek as seals and their feet were soggy.

The Halls were shut. Zac rattled the padlock on the main door.

'No point in doing that,' said Alice.

'We'd better get out of the rain.' Zac turned his face up to the sky, briefly. 'Plenty more where that's coming from. Let's go into a café and get warm.'

They had passed one just before they turned right at the lights. They ran back and ducked inside.

As Alice shook the water from her head she saw that it was quite a fancy café that they'd stumbled into, with chromium fitments and green and white veined marble table tops.

'What do you think?' muttered Zac, backing off.

'Come on, I've got enough money.'

'It's not the money,' said Zac, but he followed her. They draped their wet anoraks over the backs of their white chairs.

'Not all that comfortable, are they?' said Alice, trying to bounce up and down. But the chair was too rigid for that.

'Don't suppose they're meant to be comfortable.'

Alice nodded.

They each had a large cappuccino, and a chocolate croissant to share.

'We needed something hot,' said Alice, bringing the delicious, chocolate-speckled froth up to her lips.

'Just about bankrupted us.'

'It's an adventure, Zachary. Think of it that way!'

'I am, Allie,' he said and grinned.

As soon as they'd finished their cappuccinos they went back on the hunt. It took them another damp hour to track down the stamp fair.

The hall was packed with stands round which knots of people were gathered, their heads bent over the tables. Zac's eyes gleamed.

'We'd better not stay too long,' said Alice, 'or we won't have time to visit Lizzie.'

They spent an hour and a half at the fair. They

couldn't afford to buy much but they enjoyed seeing all the rarer and more unusual stamps.

'It's given me plenty of ideas of what to save up for,' said Alice. 'We'll do this again, shall we? Only next time I'm bringing a raincoat and an umbrella. ' Their jeans were sticking to their legs.

The rain had stopped by the time they emerged and the sun had come out.

'Now we'll steam,' said Alice. She saw her reflection in a plate glass window. Her hair was hanging in rats' tails down her back.

The next problem was finding the right bus. They walked back to the City Hall where the buses appeared to congregate. A couple of inquiries, and they were seated on the top deck of a bus being borne out to Mark and Candice's suburb.

'Posh,' said Mark, looking down at the smooth green lawns and mature, well-kept trees.

'I told you it was. They're loaded.'

'I hope they won't mind us coming.'

'They're away. In Italy. I had a postcard from Lizzie.'

'Is she on her own then with the kid?' Zac brightened.

'And her granny,' said Alice.

EIGHTEEN

The week might not have been easy for Lizzie, but Saturday was worse. Cressy had a sniffly cold and so her grandmother decreed that she should not go out, and certainly not to the sports club to swim.

'I could play table tennis,' said Cressy. 'Lizzie's teaching me.'

'You'll just do what I tell you, miss. You need a day in the house. The weather's turned. Perfect for catching colds and sore throats. And you never know what that can lead to.'

'Pneumonia,' murmured Lizzie. 'Or snake bite.'

'What's that?'

'Nothing.'

Cressy trailed round the house after Lizzie. She grizzled in her ear. She was bored. She had nothing to do. She wanted Lizzie to play *Snakes and Ladders* and *Ludo,* help her with her Lego, read to her.

'I can't read stories all day,' said Lizzie, who was bored also and longed to be able to go into her room, shut the door, lock it, plug her ears, and read a book of her own.

The rain started mid-morning. It streamed down the windows, blurring the outside world, cocooning the three of them inside four walls.

At eleven, Lizzie made a cup of milky coffee and set it on a tray with a plateful of shortbread biscuits. Then she took it through to the sitting room where Mrs Wheeler was ensconced on the settee doing her knitting. She was making a cardigan for Cressy.

'Come here a moment, child.'

Cressy hated being measured. She hated standing still. She presented her back to her grandmother, held herself stiff as a ramrod, while the piece of mustard-coloured knitting was put against her. She hated the colour of mustard, too. Lizzie sympathised with her on that count.

'I'm just about up to your armpits. Stop wriggling, Cressida! All right then, off you go. I can start casting off for the armholes now.'

Lizzie put the tray on the low, grey smoked-glass coffee table that held pride of place in the centre of the room. Candice had told Lizzie they'd brought it back from Denmark.

'I'm ready for this I can tell you,' said Granny Wheeler, reaching out for a biscuit.

As if she hadn't eaten for hours! Or had done a hard morning's work. Lizzie resolved to get out of there, even if only for half an hour. She said she'd need to go out for milk.

'There seemed plenty when I looked in the fridge earlier.'

'But Mark and Candice will be back tomorrow. And we could be doing with some bread as well.'

'Can I come?' asked Cressy.

'Granny said you should stay in,' said Lizzie quickly, before that lady would change her mind. 'Besides, it's raining. You don't want to get your feet wet.'

'Oooh,' wailed Cressy, her mouth turning into a shape like a letter-box.

'That's enough,' said her grandmother. 'You can stay with me.' She patted the settee. 'I'll teach you to knit.'

'Don't want to knit.'

'Every girl needs to know how to knit.'

'Lizzie can't knit.'

'Maybe I'll have to teach her too, then.'

Lizzie escaped upstairs to fetch her anorak. Alice could knit, and knit well. Lizzie had a vision of Alice's nimble fingers flying along the needles and the knitting growing beneath them, almost miraculously. Alice was deft in all her movements. Peter said she could be a surgeon.

Lizzie took a golf umbrella from the hall stand and let herself out. What a relief to be out! She didn't even mind the rain, in fact she rather enjoyed it, the sound of it drumming on the roof of the umbrella and the feeling of freshness it brought to the streets.

She didn't go directly to the shops but made a detour along a tree-lined avenue and up a hill. From there one had a splendid view of the roofs and spires of the city, though today they were hidden behind the curtain of rain. At a large detached house set in a spacious garden she stopped. This was where Richard lived. He'd brought her here a couple of times, had introduced her to his mother and ten-year-old sister Emma. His mother had been nice, and friendly.

Lizzie unlatched the gate and went up the drive to the front door. She rang the bell, a little nervous now. But why shouldn't she call? He called on her, at her house.

Emma opened the door. 'Oh, hi!' she said, on recognising Lizzie. 'Richard's not in.'

'He's not?' Lizzie felt her spirits droop. Not that there was any reason that Richard *should* be in. He could be at the club. 'I suppose you don't know where he's gone?'

'Mum!' Emma called back into the house. 'It's that girl Richard brought home. Lizzie. The one with the red hair. She wants to know where Richard is.'

'Doesn't matter,' said Lizzie, beginning to back away, embarrassed now.

Mrs Parker had come to the door. She was wearing gardening gloves and held a bunch of yellow roses in one hand. She must have been in the middle of arranging them.

'Oh, hello, Lizzie,' she said brightly. 'You were looking for Richard?'

'Well . . .'

'I think he said something about seeing Pam and Simon. Should I tell him you called?'

'Okay. Thanks.'

She walked back down the drive. *The one with red hair.* Had there been another one with different coloured hair? Well, why shouldn't there be? They weren't *engaged* or anything, she and Richard. The idea was ridiculous! But they had been seeing a lot of one another and she had kind of understood that they wouldn't go out with anyone else. She shook herself, sending a shower of raindrops flying from the rim of the umbrella. She was being stupid. There was probably no other girl. It was just the way Emma had phrased her sentence.

Pam lived in the next street so Lizzie thought she might as well call since she was so near. Pam's mother came to the door – she said that Pam was out, also.

'Simon came round for her about ten. They're as thick as thieves, those two! Inseparable.'

Inseparable, thought Lizzie, as she trudged up to the shops to buy bread and milk. Fat chance she and Richard would ever have to become inseparable. With Cressy standing between them. And shopping and household chores. But who'd want to be *inseparable* from another person? She could hear Alice's voice in her ear. She glanced round, almost thinking she *had* heard it. She must be going loopy. Hearing voices! What next?

She took the shopping back, made lunch and cleared up. After lunch it was Granny Wheeler's habit to take a nap on the settee. She lay on her back with her arms folded across her chest and her mouth always dropped open. They could hear her snoring from upstairs in Cressy's room where they were doing a jigsaw puzzle of *Alice in Wonderland*. Cressy had seen the jigsaw in a toy shop and bought it with her own pocket money.

'Does she look like your Alice?' asked Cressy, fitting in a piece of her face.

'A little bit. But my Alice is not so demure-looking.

So sweet-looking,' she explained, and smiled at the idea.

She wondered what her Alice would be doing today. Could be anything from digging her garden to poking around the museum downtown or lying on her stomach, head propped between her hands, reading. Alice could read for hours like that, without moving. You could step over her and she wouldn't even notice. Alice was much in her mind today, for some reason or other.

At four, Lizzie made tea. She was pouring it when Cressy, who was standing at the window gazing mournfully out, said, 'There's a big boy and a smaller girl coming up the path. And they've got carrier bags with them.'

'Who in the name could that be?' Granny Wheeler heaved herself up on to her feet and went to look She tweaked the curtain aside. She frowned. 'They look like a couple of ragamuffins. Have you ever seen them before, Cressida?'

'Don't think so.'

'They don't look as if they belong round here.'

The doorbell chimed.

'I'll go,' said Granny Wheeler. 'You never know what they could be up to. Not these days.' She left the room.

Lizzie joined Cressy at the window. By squinting sideways she could just make out the callers.

'My goodness!' she shrieked. 'It's Zac. And Alice!'

NINETEEN

'*A*lice!'

'*Frizzie Lizzie!*'

They fell into one another's arms.

'Do you know these people?' demanded Granny Wheeler.

'This is my sister Alice. And Zac from next door, Zachary Hornbeam.'

Granny Wheeler had her hands parked on her hips and was staring at them in astonishment.

'Come in!' cried Lizzie, leading the way into the kitchen, talking all the time, followed by the new arrivals, with Cressy and her grandmother bringing up the rear. 'You've no idea how wonderful it is to see you! I just can't believe it! I thought I was seeing things when I looked out the window. But how did you *get* here? And what are you *doing* here? Why didn't you let me know you were coming? Gosh, you're soaking wet, both of you!'

'We came on the train,' said Alice. 'We came for

the stamp collector's fair. We wanted to surprise you. And we got caught in the rain.'

'I'll have to get you some dry clothes. Are you staying the night?'

'The night?' echoed Granny Wheeler.

Cressy was watching Alice with rounded eyes and Alice was doing a survey of the kitchen.

'We've got to get the six train,' said Zac.

'Six!' Lizzie was disappointed. 'That doesn't give us long. Can't you take a later one?'

'Mum wouldn't buy it,' said Alice, registering the dishwasher. She'd been telling Marge and Peter that soon she'd have dishwater hands and they had made the predictable reply. Buy it yourself, madam! Why do people so often say what you think they're going to say?

Lizzie was ruminating. 'Now you can wear something of mine, Alice, even though it'll drown you. But you're longer than me, Zac. Quite a bit longer. We could borrow something of Mark's.'

'Borrow Mark's clothes?' Granny Wheeler looked horrified. She seemed to be in a state of shock altogether.

'Just temporarily,' said Lizzie. 'I'll only take something old. Nothing good. And I'll dry their wet things off in the dryer.'

Granny Wheeler found her voice. 'I don't know that you should go rummaging about in *his* wardrobe.'

'I'm sure he wouldn't mind.' He's my *father*, don't forget, Lizzie wanted to remind her. 'Follow me, guys!'

Granny remained downstairs, the others trooped up after Lizzie.

Lizzie tossed jeans and a tee-shirt at Alice and went into Candice and Mark's bedroom. Alice and Zac and Cressy waited by the door, as instructed. 'Don't want you leaving marks on their cream carpet!'

'Luxury,' said Alice, leaning in to the room from the waist. 'Definitely the lap of. You didn't exaggerate, Lizzie. Not this time.'

Opening the wardrobe door Lizzie faced a row of silken shirts and fine wool jackets. She faltered, feeling like an intruder. Perhaps he *would* mind.

'He keeps his old clothes in that bottom drawer.' Cressy pointed. 'Things he goes sailing in.'

With relief Lizzie closed the wardrobe door and yanked open the drawer. Cressy was right. She found a pair of old blue jeans with frayed cuffs and a white tee-shirt sporting a faded picture of the Hawaiian island of Maui on the front.

'Here you go, Zac! Just the job.'

With Zac suitably kitted out they went back down the stairs.

'The tea's gone cold.' Granny Wheeler was standing in the sitting room doorway with the pot in her hand.

'I'm just about to make some more, for everybody.' Lizzie took the pot from her. She felt in such high spirits that not even Granny's grumbles would be able to repress them.

'Doesn't she know how to make tea?' asked Alice, as Lizzie filled the kettle, having first closed the kitchen door.

'I've seen her make tea,' said Cressy. 'In her own house. Mummy says she's lazy.'

'Shush, you two!' said Lizzie, with a grin.

'She must think you're her maid,' commented Alice, while taking a look in the cupboards. 'Gosh, *three* cafetieres! What do they want with three? One each?'

'I don't think she likes us being here,' said Zac, who was hovering around with his arms dangling, looking as if he didn't know where to put himself.

'Pay no attention. *I* like you being here. And this is *my* home.' Lizzie saw Alice's eyes on her. 'Well, it is.'

'I didn't say anything.'

Lizzie had intended to give Alice and Zac their tea in the kitchen but Granny Wheeler came through and insisted they join her in the sitting room.

'So you're Lizzie's sister?' she said, when they were all seated on the pale blue leather suite around the grey, smoked-glass table.

'Yes,' agreed Alice politely.

'You don't look much alike.'

'That's because they've got different daddies,' said Cressy. 'Lizzie told me.'

Her grandmother didn't care for that turn in the conversation. She changed tack. 'Mind you don't drop any crumbs on the carpet, Cressida! This is a special treat for you, having your tea in the sitting room.'

Zac was already dropping shortbread crumbs and Granny Wheeler's sharp eyes had not failed to notice that. He flushed and leant over to try and pick them up. Don't worry, Lizzie told him, she'd soon run over it with the carpet-sweeper.

Alice turned an astonished eye on Lizzie. *Carpet-sweeper? Lizzie?* She'd never been known to carpet-sweep or hoover in her life, except under the pressure of dire threats. Like having her pocket money cut off. Or not being allowed to go out on Saturday night.

'So you've been at a stamp fair?' said Granny Wheeler. 'You came all the way on the train yourselves? I'm surprised your mother allowed you to, Alice.'

Lizzie knew Granny probably wouldn't be at all surprised. 'Typical of Marge,' she'd be thinking. 'Totally irresponsible mother. The type that would go off on holiday and leave their children to fend for themselves, like you read about in the newspapers. Thank goodness my Mark didn't marry *her*!'

'I'm very responsible,' said Alice, adding, 'on the whole. And Zac is getting on for sixteen.'

Zac was concentrating on his tea cup. Some tea had slopped into the saucer and he was anxious not to let any drip from the bottom of the cup on to the off-white carpet. He took a tissue out of his pocket and tried to dry the cup.

'Don't tilt it!' warned Alice.

Cressy, who was sitting on the settee leaning up against Lizzie, had gone unusually quiet.

'You okay, Cressy?' asked Lizzie.

'*You*'re not going on the train, are you?' Cressy whispered into her ear.

'Of course not! I'm staying here.'

'For ever and ever?'

'I don't know about that!'

'Nothing is for ever,' said Alice. 'That's what Peter says. My dad,' she added, for Mrs Wheeler's benefit.

Granny humphed. She didn't hold with children using their parents' Christian names, she'd told Lizzie that. Mark had never called her anything but Mother. She'd be horrified if he were to start calling her Phyllis.

Lizzie jumped up. She'd just remembered the dryer. 'I must go and see if the clothes are dry.'

'That'll be costing a fortune,' said Granny Wheeler, almost with satisfaction.

Zac set down his cup and jumped up to go after Lizzie. As he moved, his leg knocked against the edge of the grey, smoked-glass coffee table. They watched it tipping, as if in slow motion. Zac's arms flailed wildly, like the sails of a windmill, as he tried to right it, and in so doing he sent himself off balance. His other leg came up and caught the table. There was a crack like a gunshot, or the backfiring of a car. Cressy screamed.

Before them lay the table cleaved neatly in half, with the teapot, milk jug, sugar basin, and their contents heaped into the narrow valley between the two pieces. Above it all stood Zac, holding his right wrist with the fingers of his left. A deep gash seared the back of his right hand and carmine-red blood was seeping out to fall in small but steady drops on to the off-white carpet beneath.

TWENTY

'Where's the First Aid kit kept?' barked Granny Wheeler.

'In the kitchen,' said Cressy.

'Fetch it! Quickly! And some scissors. And you get me some hot water, Alice.'

Lizzie had had to sit down. The sight of blood made her feel faint. But Granny was suddenly in her element, she saw: somebody really needed her, and it was not often that anyone did.

Alice brought the water and crouched beside Zac. Granny Wheeler was holding his wounded arm firmly between her two hands.

'I'm sorry,' Zac kept saying. His face looked pallid, as if the blood was draining out of it, down through his arm into his hand. 'I've messed up the carpet.'

'That's the least of our worries!' said Granny Wheeler. 'That's a nasty looking cut you've got your-self there, lad. I'll see what I can do for you – I used to be a nurse, a long time ago. But it might have to be stitched.'

Cressy arrived with the First Aid kit and Alice swiftly took out cotton wool, lint, Dettol, gauze and a bandage. When Granny Wheeler had managed to more or less staunch the flow of blood she bent her head and examined the wound. She pursed her lips.

'It's deep, isn't it?' said Alice.

'I think we'll have to take him to the hospital.'

'I'll be all right,' protested Zac.

'All right, nothing! You'll do what you're told, lad. Now then, who's coming and who's staying?'

'I'm coming,' said Alice firmly.

'So am I,' Lizzie struggled to her feet.

'Me too!' said Cressy. 'You can't leave me.'

They piled into Granny Wheeler's little car. Zac sat in front with his arm in a sling made out of a scarf. He had been instructed to keep his hand up. There were only two seat belts in the back so Lizzie elected to be the one to sit in the middle and go belt-less.

'It's not as if we're going far,' she said.

It might not have been far but the ride over wet roads was precarious. The rain had started up again, with renewed energy. Granny Wheeler was a frightful driver. She drove as if she was in one of those telly ads, thought Alice, when a car screeches round a corniche road taking corners on two wheels. The windscreen wipers worked madly. Granny Wheeler sat tipped forward, peering through the cleared space, her white knuckles clenched over the steering wheel. All they needed was a blue light on the roof and a siren wailing. At least it would have cleared the road for them.

'I feel sick,' said Cressy, when they pulled up in front of Accident and Emergency.

No one paid any attention to her. They were too busy getting Zac out of the car.

The Accident and Emergency department was heaving with people.

'We're always busy,' said the nurse who showed them into the waiting room. 'Especially at week-ends. Traffic accidents. Falls. Sports injuries. Accidents in the home. Are you all waiting?'

'Yes,' said Alice.

'How long will we have to wait?' demanded Granny Wheeler.

The nurse could not say. 'Depends. On whether we get any emergencies in.'

'This lad is an emergency,'

'I mean heart attacks. Road accidents.'

There were not enough chairs for all of them. Zac and Granny Wheeler seated themselves, the rest leant against the wall. Around the room sat the injured, patiently nursing their wounds. Beside Zac a man with a gash on his temple was holding his face and moaning. He'd fallen on a spiked railing, said the woman who was with him, looking up from her magazine. Next to Granny Wheeler huddled a woman with her hand muffled in a bloody towel. The room was hot and stuffy and smelt of bodies and disinfectant. If you didn't feel ill when you came in, thought Lizzie, you would by the time you got out. She was not feeling too good herself. She knew she'd never make a nurse or a doctor.

The man with the gash stopped moaning for a

moment and said, 'I've been here for two and a half hours.'

'Disgraceful!' said Granny Wheeler. 'You could be bleeding to death.'

'I just about am.'

Lizzie looked at her watch. 'Ten to six.'

'We're going to miss our train!' cried Alice. She'd forgotten about time. And trains. And her mother and father awaiting her return from a day at the seaside.

'I don't know that there's much chance of getting the seven, either,' said Zac.

The man who'd been moaning was called. He lurched to his feet and followed the nurse, who told his wife to remain where she was. His departure gave the others hope.

'You never know,' said Alice. 'They might have cleared a backlog of emergencies and be getting a move on now. We might *just* get the seven, if we're lucky.' They'd need to be very lucky. But if they did get the seven then they might make it home without arousing suspicion. 'We're not far from the station here, are we?'

'Ten minutes, by car,' answered Granny Wheeler. Ten minutes by her car, at any rate.

For a while nothing seemed to happen. Nobody moved, people ceased to talk, a couple of men dropped off to sleep and started to snore, then all at once the woman with the bloody towel was taken, and after that a girl hobbling, supported by her father, and an old man who was doing his best to cough up his lungs. Three more patients arrived to take their places.

'Twenty past six,' said Lizzie, who was wondering

if she would be regarded as a deserter if she went out to get a breath of air.

'It shouldn't take long to stitch, should it, Mrs Wheeler?' asked Alice.

'They could probably do it in ten or fifteen minutes. They couldn't afford to take much more time than that, they'd never get through all this lot if they did.'

At twenty to the hour it was obvious that Alice and Zac were not going to make the seven o'clock train.

'You'll have to go and phone Mum, Alice,' said Lizzie. 'And get her to pass a message to Zac's mum while you're at it.'

Alice sighed. 'I suppose I'd better.'

'She won't be angry, not when she hears what's happened. I'll come with you.'

Cressy tagged on behind.

They had to wait in a queue in the lobby for a free phone.

'I don't know why you're looking so worried,' said Lizzie. 'You can't help it that Zac's cut his hand.'

'It's not that. I guess I'd better tell you.'

'Oh-ho!' said Lizzie, when Alice had told her tale. 'That's different. Very different. No, she's not going to like this one little bit!'

'Will Alice's mummy give her a row?' asked Cressy.

'That's an understatement!' declared Lizzie.

A phone was now free. Alice put her money in and dialled. She listened to the dialling tone.

'They're not in,' she declared. Reprieved, momentarily. She replaced the receiver, dialled again. Still no answer. 'They've probably gone to the park.'

'In this rain?'

'It might not be raining there. It's a hundred miles away.' Thank goodness! 'I'll just have to try again later. Maybe even if Zac and I were able to catch the eight . . .'

'You might get away with it?'

'There's no need to grin, Lizzie Crabtree!'

Lizzie almost opened her mouth to say 'Wheeler', then thought better of it.

They returned to the waiting room. Another lull seemed to have set in there. Lizzie put her shoulder against the wall and considered whether she would prefer to be called Crabtree or Wheeler. The first surname belonged to her stepfather, whom she'd known nearly all her life, the second to her father whom she'd known for less than a month. She came to no decision before a commotion erupted outside the window.

The glass was frosted so they couldn't see out, but it sounded as if half a dozen ambulances had arrived at break-neck speed and stopped abruptly. Tyres squealed. Doors slammed. Voices called urgently. A moment or two later the door opened and a new patient came in with his arm in a sling.

'They've got a big emergency on,' he informed the room. He appeared pleased to be the bearer of bad new. 'A bad road accident.'

A groan travelled round the room, perhaps in sympathy for the victims of the road accident, or perhaps for themselves, at the thought of the further hours they were going to have to put in on the hard chairs. Zac looked as if he might be about to topple off his.

'Lizzie, go and find some tea for Zac and me,' said

Granny Wheeler. 'We need something to help keep us alive.'

Alice, Lizzie and Cressy went to the tea machine out in the corridor and spurted dark liquid into plastic cups.

'You do realise you're not going to make the eight train now, don't you, Alice?' said Lizzie. 'You can't fool yourself any longer. You're going to have to face the music. You'll have to phone up and tell them that you're staying the night.'

TWENTY-ONE

'*W*here *are* you? Where have you been?'

The voice was so loud in her ear that Alice wondered if her mother might not be in the next room. What did she *mean*? Why was she so het up? It wasn't eight o'clock yet so they shouldn't even have begun to expect her home.

'We've nearly been up the wall. We were on the point of calling the police!'

Then it all came out. It had rained so hard at the seaside that Sharon's mum and dad had decided to call it a day at four o'clock. They'd driven back to town and as they were arriving home and turning in at their gate who should be walking past with a small child in a push-chair and another child tagging along behind but Alice's mother.

Alice groaned. Of all the luck!

'What's up?' asked Lizzie.

'That sounded like Lizzie,' said their mother at the other end of the line.

'She's going crazy,' said Alice, covering the mouthpiece with her hand.

'Better listen to what she's saying,' advised Lizzie.

Alice listened.

'So I said where's Alice and they said you hadn't been with them! What a fool I felt! There was I standing there insisting you'd gone with them and there were they saying that you'd told them you couldn't come! And then when we started to ask around it transpired that nobody had seen you *all* day.' Marge paused, to take a breath presumably, and said, 'So, where in fact *are* you, Alice?'

Alice had been waiting for her mother to ask her that.

'Well, I'm actually *in* a hospital. No, it's all right, there's nothing wrong with me. It's Zac –'

'*Zac*? What's he got to do with it?'

'He cut his hand, you see.'

'No, I don't see.'

'He cut it rather badly,' Alice went on rapidly. 'He fell on top of a glass table. We're waiting to get it stitched. We'd have been home by now if we hadn't had to wait so long. It's terrible, Mum, this Accident and Emergency department, you've no idea, you should see it, people have been sitting here for hours passing out all over the place –'

Marge cut in. 'Alice, where *is* this hospital?'

Alice told her, then stood back with the receiver held a foot from her ear and let the storm rage. What luck that Lizzie's father had ended up living so far away from their mother!

'You'll need to put more money in,' said Lizzie, reaching across to do it.

When Marge had exhausted herself, Alice said, 'I'm really sorry you've been so worried, Mum. It was just that I wanted to come and see Lizzie.'

'But you lied to me, Alice. And deceived me. And after I'd categorically forbidden you to go.'

'I know.'

'I never would have thought it of you.'

'Is Alice going to cry?' asked Cressy.

'Course not!' said Lizzie. 'Are you, Allie?'

'I want you to come straight home as soon as Zac's hand is stitched,' said Marge. 'Do you hear, Alice?'

'Yes, I hear.'

'You say Zac's hand is pretty bad?'

'It'll be all right once it gets stitched. But we can't come home straight away. We've missed the last train. We'll have to stay the night with Lizzie.'

There was silence for a brief moment, then Marge said, 'What about Mark and Candice? You know I don't like the idea of imposing on them.'

'Don't worry about that. They're not here. They've gone to Italy on business. Didn't I tell you when I got the card from Lizzie?'

'Do you mean you're all there on your *own*? Without any adults?'

'No, Granny Wheeler's here. Cressy's granny. (Alice forbore to add, Lizzie's Granny.) 'Listen, Mum, I'm about to run out of money. We've used up all our change. I'll ring you in the morning and let you know what train we'll be getting. And let Zac's mum know, will you? And tell her not to climb the wall. He's going to live.'

The phone went dead. The money had gone.

'Whew!' Alice wiped her forehead.

'At least by the time you get back tomorrow they'll have had time to calm down,' said Lizzie.

Granny Wheeler and Zac were still sitting in the waiting room. It was five minutes to nine before the nurse came in and called the name of Zachary Hornbeam. Granny got up to go with him, telling Alice to stay where she was.

'I'm the adult in charge! And I have nursing experience.' To the nurse she said, 'He's under age. I insist on accompanying him.'

They were away for half an hour. When they returned Zac had his arm in a proper sling. 'Six stitches!' he announced.

'Marked for life,' said Alice. 'It means you'll remember Candice's coffee table for the rest of your days.'

They were too tired on the return journey to care how Granny Wheeler drove. She seemed slightly less daring. No doubt she was tired too. Waiting tires you, thought Alice. Doing nothing. The three girls sat slumped in the back with Cressy half asleep between them. As they were turning into their road Granny swerved and almost knocked a boy off his bicycle.

'Stop!' cried Lizzie, sitting bolt upright. 'That was Richard.'

Granny obeyed the command and stamped hard on the brake. Alice and Lizzie were pitched forward against the seats in front.

'Honestly, Lizzie,' said Alice, rubbing the tip of her nose, 'you might have known better than to shout "Stop!" like that. We might have had to go back to Accident and Emergency.'

But Lizzie was already tugging open the door and tumbling out on to the pavement. Alice slid after her.

'Richard, are you all right?' asked Lizzie.

'I'm fine. Was that your grandmother?' He began to laugh.

'Richard, this is my sister Alice,' said Lizzie.

'Hi, Alice,' he said easily. 'I've heard a lot about you.'

'I've heard a lot about you, too.'

'Oh, really?'

He was then introduced to Zac and accompanied them home, pushing his bicycle in the gutter. Lizzie walked beside him, with the other two bringing up the rear.

'Lizzie is gullible, don't you think?' said Alice. 'Easily taken in by smoothies.'

Zac looked dejected. He was probably reflecting that smoothies knew how to avoid splitting glass tables in two and slicing their hands open.

'Never mind, Zachary,' said Alice, 'we don't have to face the music tonight. Think of that!'

When they'd all straggled in and assembled in the kitchen they realised how hungry they were.

'We missed out on supper of course,' said Lizzie. 'And it's ten o'clock.'

Zac suggested fish and chips. 'Do they have fish shops round here?'

There was one ten minutes away by bike, said Richard, and volunteered to make the run. Lizzie immediately said she'd go too; she'd borrow Candice's mountain bike from the garage. Granny Wheeler was past raising objections. She had collapsed into the rocking chair.

'So that's one, two, three, four, five fish and chips.' Lizzie counted heads. 'Granny, what about you? Do you fancy some fish and chips?'

'I don't usually like all that grease. But maybe tonight I'll make an exception. Seeing as how we've had an emergency on our hands. I'll have salt and sauce on mine and a dab of vinegar, and you might as well get me a pickled onion and a pickled egg while you're at it.'

'Might as well be hung for a sheep as a lamb,' said Alice.

'You're right!' said Granny Wheeler.

Lizzie took the remains of the housekeeping from the jar on the mantelpiece and set off with Richard.

'And don't dilly-dally on the way!' Alice shouted after them. 'Or else we might all be dead from starvation before you get back.'

Lizzie and Richard returned after forty-five minutes, claiming that there'd been a long queue at the chip shop.

'I'll bet!' said Alice, wasting no more time, starting to unwrap the brown paper parcels.

The smell, as always, was so totally overwhelming that all other considerations were put to one side. They fell on the food at once, eating with their fingers from the papers spread out on the kitchen table. Richard ladled out Coke from two monster-size plastic bottles.

So engrossed were they that they didn't hear a car pulling up in the drive or the front door opening.

Then a voice in the hall called, 'Anybody up?'

Lizzie froze, with a chip half way to her mouth. The kitchen was an absolute tip and then there was the sitting room . . . Oh my goodness! They had forgotten all about the sitting room.

The kitchen door opened, and in walked Candice and Mark, returned earlier than expected from their trip to Milan.

TWENTY-TWO

'*W*hat on earth is going on?' Candice found her voice first.

'I can explain,' said Lizzie, jumping up and almost knocking over one of the Coke bottles. Richard caught it at an angle of forty-five degrees before it went. Coke all over the floor would have been the last straw! Though maybe the last straw had already been laid.

'Is that *chip* shop fish you're eating, Cressy?' asked Candice. 'Covered in horrible greasy batter? And you know you're not allowed to drink Coke! It's not good for your teeth or your tummy.'

Cressy went on cramming fish into her mouth, in case it would be whipped away from under her.

'We were hungry,' said Granny, who had a half-eaten pickled egg in one hand and had no intention of relinquishing that either. 'We'd been at the hospital all evening.'

'The *hospital*?' said Candice. 'What *has* been going on?'

Mark was looking questioningly at Alice and Zac. 'I think some introductions might be in order, Lizzie.'

'Oh, yes, of course. You don't know Alice and Zac, do you?'

'No, I'm afraid we don't. Is this your *sister* Alice? I'd never have taken you for sisters. You don't look at all alike.'

'That's 'cos you weren't her daddy,' said Cressy.

'It's time you were off to bed,' said Candice sharply, and Cressy began to cry. 'It's way past your bedtime. Way past! Come on now!'

'Let the child finish her supper,' said Granny. 'Fish is good for the brains.'

'Did you hear me, Cressida? Up the stairs at once! And no, you can *not* finish your chips or take your Coke to bed with you!'

Candice lifted the messy paper containing the remains of Cressy's fish supper and pressing the pedal bin firmly down with her toe flung it inside. The others, all but Lizzie, carried on eating. It seemed the best thing to do. Cressy went stamping and wailing up the stairs.

'Lizzie,' said Candice, 'I think we'd better have a word with you. In the sitting room, if you don't mind.'

Lizzie did mind, of course, but there was nothing else she could do but wipe her greasy hands down the sides of her jeans and follow Candice, who had gone striding ahead. Mark brought up the rear.

Candice stopped in the sitting room doorway.

'My God!' she said.

'I can explain,' said Lizzie, for the second time.

'It had better be an extremely good explanation.' Candice's voice had chunks of ice in it.

'Good heavens!' exclaimed Mark. 'What on earth has been going on? Has there been a fight in here or something?'

Candice had gone down on her knees and was regarding at close quarters the two shards of smoked-grey glass and the spills of tea, milk and sugar on the once off-white carpet. 'And is that *blood*?'

'It was Zac. He couldn't help it. It was an accident.'

'But how did he and your sister come to be here in the first place?' asked Mark.

'They came without our permission, didn't they?' Candice rose to her feet. 'While our backs were turned. Seems like it's been Liberty Hall. No holds barred.' She looked Lizzie straight in the eye. 'I hold you totally responsible for everything that has gone on here, Lizzie. We left you in charge of Cressy and we come back to find her up at after eleven o'clock at night, eating greasy chips and drinking Coke, and the house in a state of chaos, our expensive carpet ruined, and our table split in two. I want to hear what you've got to say for yourself.'

Lizzie was aware that the lid on top of her head was rattling and about to fly off. Underneath she was building up enough steam to run a railway engine.

'What do you think I am?' she cried. 'An unpaid au pair girl? You've expected me to look after Cressy morning, noon and night. To give up anything I want to do so that you can do anything you want. You've not treated me like a daughter in the house!

You've exploited me. You've treated me like a skivvy!'

'So that's all the gratitude we get!' said Candice. She turned to Mark. 'We give her a lovely room, feed her, make her welcome, I give her clothes, and she turns round and spits in our faces!'

'Lizzie,' said her father helplessly.

'But don't you see, Mark?' appealed Lizzie, who had calmed a little. 'I've not been treated like a daughter. No daughter of my age would be expected to take complete charge of a sister of seven all day and every day.'

Candice answered for him. 'Would they not? In my experience families pull together and help one another. But quite obviously *you* have not been raised in the same ethic.'

'I'd like to see you making your sister's breakfast, lunch and tea every day!' said Lizzie, knowing she was going to lay herself open to a charge of impertinence on top of everything else, and not caring. Or caring rather, but knowing her boats were burnt and that there was not much more to be lost. 'I'd like to see you ironing her clothes, taking her swimming, reading to her –!'

'I think that's enough, Lizzie,' said her father quietly.

'Perhaps we're seeing her in her true colours, Mark. And perhaps that's not such a bad thing.'

She never has liked me, thought Lizzie. She just put up with me.

Lizzie was lying on her bed weeping when Alice came in to the room.

'You had to tell her, Lizzie! You couldn't keep it in any longer.' Alice had heard the row from the kitchen where they had been sitting with the door open. They had all heard it. 'You couldn't go on pretending to be somebody you weren't. And they *were* exploiting you.'

'Her. Not him.' Lizzie sat up, snuffling.

'No, him, too. He might not have meant to, but he was. That's just as bad, as far as I can see. End result's the same.'

'I've disappointed him. He didn't say so, not in so many words, but I could tell from the way he looked at me. I didn't want to disappoint him, Alice. I wanted to please him. To make him proud to have me as his daughter.' Lizzie gulped. 'And I've messed the whole thing up.'

'*You* didn't mess it.' Alice took two tissues from the box and put them into Lizzie's hand.

Lizzie blew her nose. 'Yes, I did. And now I've got to leave here and I'll probably not see him again and that'll be the end of that. I wish I'd never come in the first place.'

'No, you don't. You've seen him now, you know who he is.'

'Maybe it'd have been better to have left him as he was.'

'In your dreams? Things don't always stay there though, do they? I mean sometimes they seem to slip out of your dream and get mixed up in your life. Real life.' Alice yawned. 'I'm exhausted. Can we go to bed? I'll have to sleep with you. Is there room?'

'There's room. Where's Zac sleeping?'

'Mark's made him up a bed in his study.' Alice was already under the downie. 'Mum and Dad'll be pleased to see you back, anyway.'

'I can't go back there! After walking out like that! Mum and I'd be at one another's throats in no time. That's another scene I've messed up.'

'What else can you do? Go to London and sleep in a cardboard box? Bit cold in the winter. You could get hypothermia.'

'I might go to Aunt Lucy's. You know I get on well with her.' Lucy was Marge's sister. She lived alone, was childless, and good fun.

'Mum would be upset.'

'But how can I go back home?'

'By swallowing your pride,' Alice was going to say, but was overtaken by sleep.

TWENTY-THREE

'Lizzie, I want to talk to you,' said Mark, looking at Alice.

Alice vanished.

Mark took the chair beside the table and turned to face Lizzie, who was sitting on the bed gazing at her knees.

'Do look at me!' He reached out and touched her arm. 'That's better. You've been crying! Well, no wonder. I'm sorry, Lizzie. Listen, Candice and I have been talking and we realise that things were a bit het up last night, what with you having to cope with Zac's hand and go to the hospital. And perhaps we have expected a little too much of you. We're prepared to give it another go, if you'd like to try. Would you?'

'Don't know.'

'I'd have to ask you first of all though to apologise to Candice. You said some pretty harsh things to her, and she has been generous to you.'

'But it's true! That I've been treated like an au pair!'

'Is that so very bad? Au pair girls are meant to live like family. We've always treated our au pairs well.'

He doesn't see, thought Lizzie dully. He doesn't see the difference. He thinks that if I apologise to Candice everything in the garden will be lovely. Or at least all right. But Candice won't think that. She's sharper than he is, she sees things for what they are, and she sees me as filling the role of an pair girl. If their au pair girl hadn't left Candice would never have let me come and stay. It was *she* who let me, I see that now. He just goes along with what she wants.

Lizzie looked up at her father. She couldn't say what he wanted her to say, to smooth everything over. He wanted to go on with his life and have it disturbed as little as possible. He always had.

'Why *didn't* you stand by my mother?' she asked quietly.

'What's that got to do with this?'

'Everything! It's why I'm here, now. It's why all this has happened. You loved her, you said you did.'

'I was young —'

'You've said that too.'

'Lizzie, I don't see any point in us going on with this.' He stood up.

Yes, run off, she thought, when things get tricky. That's what you usually do.

'But do think over what I said, Lizzie,' he said. 'About staying. I'd still like you to stay.' And he left her.

He wanted her to stay. Was that enough to hold her?

'Lizzie, can I come in?' Cressy was her next visitor. She came in without waiting for an answer and dropped on to the bed beside her. 'Alice says you're going away. Please don't go, Lizzie! Please *don't!* I couldn't bear it if you went. I wouldn't have anyone of my own.'

'You've got your mummy and daddy.'

'But they're not here all day. And you're my best friend.'

'I wouldn't be here all day either once school started.'

'We'd both go to school. And you could meet me afterwards and look after me. I want you to stay. You're my sister – you said you were!'

'Yes, I am your sister. And I want you to remember that.'

'Please then, Lizzie!'

'It's not so simple.'

'Cressy!' called Candice from downstairs. 'Come down, please! Your breakfast is on the table.'

'Promise!' Cressy seized Lizzie's hands.

'I can't promise, I'm afraid, dear. I'll have to see.'

Cressy went out, and Alice came in. 'There's an inter-city at eleven. I asked Candy Floss if I could use the phone and I rang home to tell them Zac and I'll be on it. I said you might be too.' She waited for a response from Lizzie. 'They said they hoped you would be.'

'One BLT and one tuna salad,' said Zac, laying them on the table. 'Take your pick. That's all I'd money for. Jolly expensive, railway food.'

166

'I'm not particularly hungry,' said Lizzie, who was looking pale and rather limp.

'I am.' Alice began to peel the cling film off the bacon, lettuce and tomato.

'You eat an awful lot for your size, Allie,' commented Zac.

'It goes to her brains,' said Lizzie with a weak smile.

Alice bit into her sandwich. 'You okay?' she asked.

'I guess.' Lizzie sighed and her lip trembled a little.

Alice squeezed her arm. Zac shuffled his feet and looked out of the window.

'How did it go, the farewell scene?' asked Alice.

'All right, I suppose. He said we could meet sometimes. Not in his house of course. Though he didn't say that, not in so many words. But I know *she* wouldn't want me. She'll feel she's given me a chance and I've blown it.'

'She likes to feel she's in the right. How will you see him, then?'

'He said he'd drive over and we could spend the day together and he'd bring Cressy. Doubt if he'll come more than a couple of times a year. It'll slip his mind. He's so busy with other things.'

'He's a bit, kind of, on the surface.' Lizzie glared and Alice went on, 'Well, he is, isn't he? Not deep. Not overly, anyway. Though I'm sure he's not a bad man.'

'No, he's not. I'm sure he means well.'

'That's not the same as doing well.'

'So he's not a saint. Who is?'

'Don't look at me!' Alice finished her sandwich.

'Oh, okay, he's selfish!'

'They both are. Poor Cressy.'

'I'm going to keep in touch with her. I'll ask Mum if she can come and stay sometimes.'

'The house will be bursting at the seams.'

'She can share my room.'

Which room was that? wondered Alice, but did not voice the question. Time enough to raise it when they got home.

'Did you say goodbye to Mr Smoothie Richard?' she asked.

'I rang him up. We got on really well when we were together. We had a good time.' Lizzie's tone was defensive. 'He's a very nice boy. Just because you wouldn't fancy him!'

'I certainly wouldn't,' agreed Alice.

'I'm going to miss him.'

'Only for a couple of days.'

'Anyone want the tuna?' asked Zac.

Lizzie shook her head. 'I said goodbye to Granny Wheeler too. She's not so bad, you know. In small doses. If you stand up to her.'

'I saw her kissing you!' said Alice.

'She's asked me to come and spend a week-end with her. I thought I might. She is my –'

'Grandmother, after all,' concluded Alice.

Peter was waiting at the station.

'Welcome back,' he said to Lizzie and gave her a warm hug. He held up his hand to silence her. 'Now you don't have to start saying you're sorry! We all are. We're just pleased you've come home.'

'Do I have to say I'm sorry?' asked Alice. 'Or are

you pleased to see me as well? Can I be part of the amnesty?'

'*You*! Don't you ever do that to us again!'

'Promise,' said Alice. 'Brownies, honour.'

'You were never a Brownie, were you, Allie?' said Zac.

Marge was at home laying the table for a family meal in the dining room. They usually only ate in the dining room on high days and holidays, Christmases and birthdays. Alice retreated to the kitchen to let them get their reunion over with in peace. Maybe not peace exactly, but undisturbed by any other human being.

When Marge and Lizzie came in to the kitchen they had their arms linked. Their eyes were red, and they were laughing.

'We've resolved to make a new start,' said Marge.

'Is that a turkey you've got in there?' asked Alice, straightening up from the oven.

'Just a small one.'

'To celebrate the return of the prodigal daughter!' said Alice.

They had a good meal, a bit like Christmas, as Lizzie said, with candles and flowers, and Jamie, who'd been allowed to come to the table instead of sitting in his high chair, spilt his orange juice only once. After they'd eaten Peter took the two boys out to work off their energy in the garden.

Alice and Lizzie sat on round the table with their mother. She was feeling relaxed and mellow after a couple of glasses of red wine.

'Lizzie and I are determined to make things work better from now on, aren't we, Lizzie?' she said. 'It won't always be easy, of course, we know that. I daresay we'll still have our little spats.'

'I daresay.' Lizzie grinned.

'As long as they're little,' said Alice.

'Mum's going to start art classes in the autumn! She's enrolled for two afternoons a week!'

'You've not, Mum, have you?' said Alice. What about the boys?'

'I've arranged a child-minder.'

'Well!'

Candice! thought Alice. She'd be willing to bet her boots that it was the thought of Candice that had galvanised their mother into action. Well, at least Candy Floss had come in useful for something.

'That reminds me, Alice,' said her mother. 'Sharon.'

'I don't know why it should remind you. It's a bit of a jump. But I thought we were having an amnesty. Can I have another piece of pie?'

'Help yourself. I wasn't going to start on you. No, I was just thinking what a nice girl Sharon was.'

'And what a nice friend she would make for me?' Alice put a spoonful of cream on top of her plum and apple pie. Her favourite pudding.

'Well, why not? You should have friends of your own age.'

Lizzie pretended to saw away on an imaginary violin.

'I thought Sharon seemed very agreeable.' Marge was not going to give up. Her two daughters knew that she operated on the principle that if she hung on long enough she would wear you down eventually. 'It wouldn't kill you to spend some time with her, would it now?'

'Don't suppose it would. Not kill me outright. Might bore me *half* to death, though.'

'Honestly, Alice!' Marge poured herself another glass of wine. 'That's not very charitable of you.'

'You're driving your mother to drink!' said Lizzie.

'I was thinking you might like to ask her to tea.'

'But what would I talk to her about, Mum?' demanded Alice.

'There must be something, for goodness sake! You're on your own far too much.'

'That's not true! I've got heaps of friends. As many as I've got time for. I'm far too *busy* to take on any more. I've got Mr Gibbon and Mrs Moon and Khalil and Mr O'Friel. And then there's Zac. He takes up quite a bit of time.' Alice paused, and added with a grin, 'And I've got Lizzie, now that she's returned to the fold. I won't have to give my room back, though, will I?'

'It's *my* room,' protested Lizzie.

'You left it! So it's mine now.'

'But that was just while I was away.'

'No taking back – we agreed!'

'You little –!'

'Girls, girls!' cried their mother.